had avoided most of those issues his entire life and he couldn't say he was proud of that, more, he was thankful. When a guy looks successful, everybody wants a piece of him. It don't matter if they didn't earn it, They just want it because they think he has it, they should too. Let them put their butts out there on the line and make it happen. Jake did. He earned every dime of what he stole and no one could prove otherwise and he liked it that way. Just keep your sticky little fingers out of his loot and Jake wouldn't have to do something to you that neither of you would like. Jake wasn't violent, but he was very protective of what was his. He didn't like folks to come nosing around. He was kind of particular that way as anyone might be. Jake was serious about his business. It was the only way anyone should be about what made their money for them.

And he never stayed in a town where he'd done business. If he was there for ten minutes, he was late for the door. That's why he would come into to town, case a joint or a person and maybe stay a few days to make the arrangements, make something he wanted his and POOF! Like magic he was gone before they even knew something had happened. That's why Jake was the best. He kept things cool; he kept things light and he kept on moving so that no one ever suspected; until he was gone and it was too late. But most of all, he always tried to keep from actually breaking the law; mostly. Or at least make it appear that way. More than one local yokal or FBI agent had been left scratching their head wondering how he'd pulled the wool over everyone's eyes and left them with nothing to charge him. That's the part he liked the best, when they knew he'd taken them all to the cleaners but they couldn't figure out what law he had broken.

Today wasn't much different, Jake had come into Dallas in a nondescript ten-year old beige Chevy Caprice that no one thought to notice. He checked in at the Motel Six on Market Center Boulevard knowing it was used mostly for prostitution and drug running. He could hang low and just look like anyone else at this place. The hotel management knew what was going on there, but they turned a blind eye because the occupancy rates were near 100% from 'innocent' long-term clientele. No one could prove otherwise and as long as everyone kept their noses clean, the po-po turned a blind eye. The cops were like that. Very few actually cared about the law these days, they just wanted their piece of the pie. It likely had always been that way but it was not up to the news sources to report the truth, only the narrative they were told to report. Jake felt safer here than at the Mariotte because no one dared look anyone else in the face. Nobody would ever finger him and he paid a week in advance with cash.

The beige Chevy Caprice he'd bought a few miles East near the town of Mesquite from a Good Enough inventory at the Nissan dealership for cash using a fake ID, fit right in. They never checked ID on cash deals for old cars; shoot, they counted on the Mexican wholesalers to do the same so no one really cared. Jake would use it for now, thirty days, maybe more and dump it at some convenience store parking lot or such when he left town on a Greyhound bus. Sometimes he just parked a vehicle on the street near a bus station. It would take a week for anyone to report it to have the po-po tow it and they'd be checking with the previous owner to find that it had been traded in. They'd look for maybe as much as another week only to come to a dead end. If it wasn't such a brain dead plan it would be genius using the failed system. Jake did pat himself on the back for that scam, no one was ever able to trace him even if he got a ticket. He'd show the official bill of sale and the fake ID being from the United Kingdom, no one could even track him on the ticket. He thought that maybe when he retired, he could go into making fake IDs for others. It took only a little skill and as long as the cover story was solid, it worked every time, except at airports, nothing much worked at airports anymore. So, Jake avoided those like the plague. Passports were especially tough at the airports. He left those to others more skilled at the art.

This was going to be a special job and it would require some finessing. Jake didn't like to use a fence because that was like having a partner, just another mouth to blab or point a finger or rip him off. That's why Jake preferred to work with cash, steal cash, hoard cash, spend cash and that is why he had to make as much cash as he could before society went cashless. He had to admit, debit cards would be nice to use, fairly convenient, but so easy to track everything one did. It was ridiculous that people lived their lives on a piece of plastic allowing the government to know their every move. He just didn't understand how people could be so blind.

This job had to be big and it involved the trust he had to instill in a very rich woman who also liked cash. In fact, the rumors were heavy and quite certain that she kept several million in cash on hand and he'd need to find out where and how to access the money. Mrs. Ida Periwinkle was no fool and jake was sure she would smell a con from a mile away so he wasn't going to try to play the rich playboy as he had done so many times in the past.

So many older women desperate for companionship would fall to that heartbreaking ruse and he was good at it. It wasn't something he liked doing to them as it usually left them devastated; but, in a pinch. He preferred a straight forward burglary after learning the secrets of the security system and then disappearing into the mist of a full moon. He was going to do what he never, ever did and be himself; but with a different name of course so, not quite himself. At least this time the mark would not be an older woman but rather a very good-looking younger woman and the roll would be much easier to play. If this worked out, he wouldn't feel like vomiting in the back of his mouth when he kissed her. She was still ten years his senior but it didn't show and she still knew how to get down with the Dallas nightlife. If he wasn't still looking to remain single, he might have wanted to go for this woman on a more permanent basis.

Jake had spent countless hours researching every aspect of Ida's life and history. Not just where she grew up and who her family and friends were but right down to her favorite foods, drinks, colors, clothing designers, nail polish and her perfume. He had it all in his head and he felt as if he knew her personally already. He had to know these things if he was to stay on schedule to be done in a month and dump his car but he also knew that this plan might be too far over the top aggressive.

Wooing a younger woman was much harder than wooing an older woman. Not only did they have choices but they had friends that older women don't have. Friends, male and female would stop at nothing to destroy any chance of him getting close to her if they could. The women, either out of jealousy or concern for her wellbeing and the men out of competition for her good looks and wealth. This was a play he'd not done before; he'd not wanted to take the chance of falling for someone and he quite honestly, didn't like the pain he might visit on the mark. It was tough to be a con man with a conscience, that's why he preferred the straight forward burglary. In, out and gone before any feelings were overly involved.

Ida was smart and no one knew exactly where she kept her cash. She had investments that kept money in her bank accounts but she was not one to trust the banks or the feds. Before her husband had died, he taught her very well in the ways of the financial sector and she was pretty savvy of her own accord even before that. She liked keeping plenty of money on hand for those times when some IRS agent or States Attorneys General might decide to freeze her assets for whatever reason. In this day and age Jake couldn't blame her for that and he was hoping to take full advantage of that fact. Money was such a liquid thing, it could flow right out of her hands and into his, all he had to do was to find the valve that would open the flood gates.

First things first, Jake wanted to find a clothier with some style. He had a tendency to travel light so he didn't always keep a wardrobe with him The last town he'd had to get out of even quicker than usual. There was no trail for that one-horse-town sheriff to chase him down but had he been caught, it would have meant a ten year sentence and that just wasn't in Jake's plan for the immediate future. He'd walked away with the cash of another con man, but that con man owned the sheriff and Jake had dried up the well to the sheriff's future fortunes. Needless to say, that good old boy wasn't any too happy with him. Sheriffs were almost always the hardest to pervert because of their deep respect for the law and the constitution. Every now and then he ran into one that had no inkling of what the constitution or the law meant to most people. That man had been one to stay away form had he known in advance.

Jake on the other hand, felt like he'd done a good deed putting that grifter out of business. He'd been bilking the town's people for a decade with the sheriff's help and those two thought they'd be running high on the hog for a good many years to come. Instead, the sheriff had no one to blame but his partner or they'd both be going to jail. Another one of those partner situations Jake didn't like. So, North on the Dallas North Tollway to the Shops at Legacy. It was time to look the part he would be playing and the needed to spend some jack to make that happen.

He didn't want to spend a fortune, he wasn't trying to look like big money, just more than the average Joe. Travis Mathew, Urban Outfitters and The Impeccable Pig were among his first stops and then maybe a few more before getting dinner at one of the many somewhat advanced culinary establishments he'd looked at online. Ya, that online thing, it had it's uses. Jake was a bit of a foody as his budget and his pallet weren't inclined to McDonalds; although once in a blue moon he just couldn't resist a little Kentucky Fried Chicken.

Ida Periwinkle had come from a minor amount of new money but everyone knew she had married old man Periwinkle for his fortune. But she treated him right and he'd died happy, albeit young, at the age of 69 by a federal agent's gun, so it was well accepted that she'd done right by him. She didn't try to take from his 2 kids, Ilene and Max IV, she graciously accepted what they'd all agreed upon together and everyone lived peaceably. No one could argue the intentions of anyone else and the lawyers and courts were disappointed there was no court battle on which they could all make a bit of money. Although word was, the three of them were not exactly one big happy family, they got along. Not any of Jake's business anyway but he liked to know what it was he was walking into.

During his shopping spree, Jake noted there was a lot of female talent in this part of the city and most of them were blonde. He'd always found it strange that blonde women were held in such high esteem amongst the ilk that liked to show their wealth that most of them didn't really have. It was Jake's experience and well-founded opinion that most people tried to put on airs and climb the social ladder of acceptance by having the right wives, the right cars, the best-looking children and homes well beyond their income. It was no different here and maybe even more so as this was the big city of Dallas, and the surrounding areas, and people here were trying to make contacts, shake the right hands and generally hob knob their way into positions of betterment. That's why he would be able to fit right in. He already had the money, he had the looks, he didn't need the right car. He would rent one if he did and his personality was what would make him shine. He was a bit arrogant about his shining personality.

Jake had the ability to charm the pants off a nun and he'd do just that if he had to. After finding just the right attire to say to the elites of the city that he was on his way, he decided to stop into a little eatery known for its healthy entrées and decadent deserts. It was a bit of an oxymoron in diet but it was so nice to treat himself with such fair. It was his guilty pleasure. This evening it was a pasta salad heavy on red onions, black olives, cherry tomatoes, a bit of bacon and olive oil among other little delights. Followed by a delectable creamy smooth slice of three-layer cake with embedded peach pieces and strawberry frosting and yes, real strawberries. It was heaven and Jake wanted the whole cake but of course, that couldn't happen and keep his boyish figure. That had not been a problem for Jake until he hit twenty-five but these days, he needed to watch those things if he wanted to be desirable. He had the looks and the charm but he'd lose all appeal once he had a muffin top or a beer belly.

Time to go back to the room and deal with his new clothing. He'd remove the tags and launder everything such that even looking new they wouldn't have the new clothes folds in them. That reminded him, he needed to get laundry supplies including dryer sheets. Those dryer sheets made everything smell so nice and if there was one thing that turned a lady's head, it was a good smelling man. He managed to snag his toiletries before racing out of the last town so he had most of what he needed where that was concerned. By the time he got back to the room it was already after ten. One thing he wouldn't do is go out to do laundry this time of night in this neighborhood. This neighborhood wasn't too terribly bad during the day, but he wouldn't take chance after dark. He was trained and he certainly could take care of himself, but he didn't need any police attention. Tomorrow was another day.

One thing about these cheap hotels, they didn't skimp on anything but the essentials. That's why Jake liked to carry his own soap, shampoo, coffee, creamer and even his own coffee maker. Those single cup makers were for the birds; grackles to be specific. He often brought his own toilet paper as well. Something about punching through that single ply stuff just didn't make him happy. Time to turn off his brain and get some shut eye. Punching through, what made him think of that? Eew!

It was time to surreptitiously bump into Ida. His information put her at Arthur's Steakhouse in Adison most Friday nights. A lot of the wanna-be highbrows spent time there because it was actually a very nice place, the food was truly excellent and the aquariums were incredible to view while eating. They had a small dance floor and the prices kept the low-end riff raff away. Tomorrow he could start phase one, flirting for a phone number and then ghosting her.

But not for long, that was the key to gaining a foothold of trust. he'd wait for four days and then call to let her know how he was at his mother's funeral. How sorry he was for not letting her know sooner. Even if he had to leave a message, the trust would grow, especially when he came back with a funeral leaflet with his mother's supposed photo, the address of a real church, a real funeral and a real dead woman; he'd already found one in Austen, just the right distance away that no would think to go and confirm anything. Jake was ready to rock and roll tomorrow night! His name would be Charles Gordon, sister Allissa and his mother, Mellissa Gordon. The story was straight and now to put out the bait.

CHAPTER TWO:
BAITING THE HOOK

Jake rose early to get a jump on all the stay-at-home house wives and single mothers with young children that would flood the local laundromat by eight o'clock. He'd still be there when they arrived, much to his chagrin, but he'd have his clothes in the dryer already and only have to fold them, pack up and leave. He hated dealing with the screaming kids and the frustrated with their lives mothers, with curlers in their hair, wishing they'd married a rich man that could afford a washer and dryer or a man that at least worked. He really wanted a second cup of joe before going but he could warm that up in the microwave when he got back to the room. A true coffee aficionado would chide him for such a travesty of decorum, but there were none staying in his room; in spite of his wanting to be that way himself. The tags gone from his haul yesterday, he had the laundry basket filled with his 'dirty' clothes, detergent, fabric softener and dryer sheets. He was out the door of his room and loaded into the Caprice way too early. Oh, how he wished he could have a few more sips of coffee.

Walking into the laundromat there was that distinct smell of chlorine bleach and detergent perfumes dominant in all of these low-brow establishments. It hit him in the face like seeing an unwelcome acquaintance walking his direction, unavoidable and imminent. He set about his labor with the mechanical efficiency he had learned as a child helping his own mother do the same automatic motions she had taught him over thirty-five years ago. He missed his mother. She wasn't the ideal mom that most kids would wish for, but she had taken care of him first and foremost even before her smoking, drinking and drug habits took their inevitable toll on her existence.

She was not a junky but the pot made her a different person just as the alcohol had and even though she was his mother in the mornings, she was someone he didn't know by early afternoon. A beautiful woman in her younger days, she always attracted the wrong kind of attention from men and because of her social and financial standing she was always surrounded by men of a nature that precluded an acceptable standard of living. She didn't seem to know how to break away from that life no matter how much Jake had encouraged her. He never liked any of the men she brought home to meet him and he eventually came to detest that type of person male and female. They, men and women, always ran together and somehow ended up staying until all hours of the night keeping him awake until they all finally passed out. Jake would have to pick his way through the living room filled with the bodies, usually of strangers, that had ended up sleeping on the living room floor. His mother, however, was always awake and had breakfast ready for him regardless. Even if it was only eggs and buttered toast or oatmeal. It helped to dampen the embarrassment he felt for her and it showed him that in spite of all of her many faults, she loved him more than her friends and her habits and saw to his needs from that very love. Regardless of anything else, she loved him and he loved her for that.

She had been one of these very women with children in the laundromat that he strived so much to avoid. It always brought back memories of his childhood he'd worked so hard to escape, and for the most part he had. The laundromats, this one detail of his intrepid childhood was the last vestige of where he had originated and it weighed upon him like the proverbial anchor or mill stone around his neck. This job should be his last and he would be done with the chicanery he had come to perfect for his survival and advancement into a young retirement. He hoped he would never have to step foot into the memories of his youth again. Not that they wouldn't occur, but they would occur only by his choice. He would be able to go back to the Louisiana house just outside the swamp lands that was now little more than a place bums and drug addled losers flopped. He would dig up the tin boxes of cash he'd buried under that house and put their contents into a wall safe in a mansion of his own and raze the place. His cabin in Arkansas he would keep but he wouldn't need it anymore.

While laboring over his memories, Jake had finished his work at the laundromat and was loading his clothes into the Caprice. It was time to go back to the hotel and hang up tonight's attire, catch some second-rate movie on the hotel cable network and probably nap a good part of the day. It could be a late night and he wanted to be as fresh mentally as his freshly laundered clothes. His plan was to wear his black silk shirt with the sleeves rolled up over a pair of just lighter than black trousers and a woven leather belt with a gold clasp for easy adjustment. He wondered if a tie would be in order but then decided that would be a bit much for a meeting of happenstance. After all, he didn't want it to appear that he was there fishing for a mate. Just a great single guy out for some dinner and a little entertainment for the evening.

The first thing one noticed when walking into Arther's were the huge aquariums built into the wall behind the bar. They appeared to be at least two-hundred-fifty fifty gallons each. They were filled with colorful fish of which Jake was not familiar. Then one was struck by the natural wood grain of all the accoutrements that appeared to be finished in a high sheen spar varnish or some such thing. The main dining room however was painted all in a high gloss white that set an expectation to be very clean and high born. The lowered glow but fully sufficient lighting and the light fixtures were of obvious taste. Then, he noticed how many tables they had crowded into such a small area in front of the bar although the main area was relatively open. There was a hardwood dance floor they had exposed for the enjoyment of the evening crowd and albeit small, it was sufficient for shaking one's butt. It was certainly a decent enough place and Jake could understand the draw it had for the desperately seeking companionship crowd that would more than likely be gracing it's tills with cash and credit cards most every night it was open. Tonight was no different and he was here to take advantage of that very atmosphere.

Jake ordered the Jumbo Lump Crab Louie with Avocado and Remoulade as the drinks he would be having would suffice for his carbohydrate intake. Avocados were always a welcome addition to any menu item and he just couldn't pass on crab, real or faux. He hoped that for the price, it was real. The after-dinner evening crowd was just now starting to filter in so Jake was happy he'd gotten his order in in time to beat the rush. Most of them would likely be like him and ordering light but no matter the restaurant, a rush always put things behind. It could still be hours before Ida showed if she showed at all so Jake would have to temper his alcohol consumption and it would be bad judgement to be even slightly inebriated on a first meat and great. As his research showed, Ida was prone to having a good time but there was no indication she was in the habit of over indulging.

There were many single women dressed to the hilt this evening and Jake couldn't help but lick his chops at all the talent he was seeing. It was amazing what Dallas had to offer and a great deal of that was because of all the oil and tech money that filtered into this town and even this state in general. Texas, Like Florida had no state income tax so it drew the very best attorneys, executives, upper managers and successful small businessmen and they always married well and had beautiful sons and daughters. It was a town ripe for the picking but he had to keep his mind on the prize and she was a prize herself in the realm of all the beauties against which she was in competition. That's why Jake's game had to be right on the mark. He was very handsome and a naturally likeable guy anyway, but to catch this woman, he would need to be by nature everything she ever wanted.

It was getting a bit later than he would have expected but Ida finally made an appearance and what an appearance that was! It started at her feet with black open strapped shoes that wound laces all the way up to her knees, something akin to what a stripper might wear but with heals only at most, an inch and a half high. Not the most comfortable but suitable for dancing on this tiny floor. Her tan nylons were of a shade that didn't betray the skin tone of her fully exposed arms and face while her black sequined dress was split up the right side to expose plenty of leg while not being slutty. The dress ended in a deep v cut neck and wider shoulder covers that extended just short of her actual shoulders. It made her shoulders appear wider than what they were without over accentuating them and left them temptingly bare. She wore black onyx earrings that dangled just a bit and her shoulder length black hair was angle cut to flow down in the front. She was most certainly a vision of beauty and grace and her physical motion flowed lasciviously. She was a vision of heaven on earth and Jake was taken more than he expected.

Their eyes met as she scanned the room and as she purposely looked away Jake could see her smile just the tiniest smile in approval of what she saw. She might have an interest in making his acquaintance. It was his experience that if he didn't make an immediate move, she would realize he didn't have the huevos to be worth her while and he'd never have that opportunity a second time. He got up and went to her table without hesitation and introduced himself as Charlse Gordon, in town to consider buying a property. That identified him as someone with means and the ability to do business. He then had to dangle the bait.

"I couldn't help but notice you as you walked in, and please don't take this the wrong way but you are absolutely stunning and I'd like to get to know you a bit if you wouldn't mind."

ABOVE THE LAW REALTY

"I don't generally entertain the thought of having out of town friends but you have made your own impression on me so please, have a seat. If I don't like you, I'll just excuse myself."
Said with a smile and a bit of a laugh, it was obvious to Jake that she was trying to play a bit of hardball with some guy that just walked up and hit on her, testing his metal as it might be.
"I just tried Arthur's here as a friend of mine back in Louisiana recommended it. I was not disappointed. Is this your first time here?"
"I've been a few times and have never been disappointed," Jake knew that wasn't exactly true as this was one of her favorite haunts. It was likely she didn't want to appear to be a night owl on the prowl.
At that moment a very tall and debonair gentleman in a suite about fifty-five or sixty years old walked in with some thirty-year-old honey attached to his arm and he nodded and said, "Good evening, Ida." He didn't bother to introduce his date and they walked on.
"Okay, busted. Maybe more than a few times. I've met some people from around town at one time or another."
"Hardly an issue. Once a person finds a place they like, it's easy to make friends, I'm sure. Would you allow me to buy you a drink?"
"Thank you, a Gimlet please?"
"I'll be right back."

Jake was surprised that there were no servers available to get their drinks at an establishment like this but he wasn't the type to complain about it. The bartender was quick and Jake paid in cash anyway. The bartender gave him a look of disgust when Jake gave him only two dollars for the two drinks but what did he expect? It wasn't Jake's job to put the bartender's kids through school. Jake had a similar experience at a blue Martini near Phoenix, Arizona at one time. The bartender refused to serve him after he tipped a dollar for her to reach into a bucket of ice to give him an eight-dollar Voss water. Trash is as trash does and Jake wasn't afraid to say so. If the bartender gave him any grief he'd take care of it in a much more defined manner. He walked the gimlets back to the table where another man was hitting on Ida. Jake had not been gone that long and he didn't really care that Ida was entertaining the man although to her credit, she had not allowed him to sit in the chair Jake had been occupying. He slid in and supplied one of the drinks to Ida in a smooth motion of which a dancer would be proud. The other gentleman taking the hint excused himself and Jake didn't even open the subject, he just asked Ida if the gimlet was to her liking.

"Oh, yes. They do a great job of making it taste good and knocking one's socks off as well. Some places will try to make it sweet and they end up adding too much Lime mixer. They mix it fifty/fifty here and that's the way it's meant to be done."

Jake liked this woman's taste on that point maybe she would be an enjoyable mark and he wouldn't have to work too hard to enjoy his time with her.

"So, Charles, what is your line of work?"

"Oh, a bit of this and a bit of that. I invest in precious metals; I play in the market just a smidge and have some rental properties. Nothing too big, a small three-story office building and a few four plex's in Shreveport, a few single-family dwellings here in the Dallas area."

"Oh, so your independently wealthy?"

"I'm not to that point yet, as the bank still owns a couple of my houses here, but I don't worry about money either. I guess one could color me comfortable. What about yourself? Any trades or hobbies?" Jake already knew the answer to this question but he wanted to see what Ida would tell him.

"I married well and his kids were not terribly greedy when he passed. He left me an apartment complex and a bit of cash so I guess you could say I'm in the same boat as yourself. Mostly I'm looking for some investments but Dallas is growing so quickly everyone is snapping them up faster than I can get to them."

Well, she wasn't totally honest and Jake couldn't blame her but the basic story checked out with what he knew.

"I am not looking for a partner but I'd be happy to ask my source if he's got anything that he could recommend for you."

"That would be wonderful, I'd really appreciate that!"

"I'm going to get out of here as I have to get up early to meat Jim at the first property, but if you would care to give me your number, I'll pass it along to Jim."

"Well, aren't you the slick one. Do me a favor and get my number at the same time."

"I hope you can understand, it really is for Jim but If you're not opposed to it, may I give you a call as well?"

"Of course you may, but don't leave me hanging to long, your competition walked in tonight and I might just give him a chance."

"Oh, no! I'm so worried!" Wink, Wink, "Very good to meet you, Ida."

"Like wise, Charles, I look forward to hearing from you and Jim, both."

Jake's time that evening was well spent and he got away cheap, Ida was not an easy mark and he'd have to be overly convincing with his plan to have a relative die. Not to mention finding an old friend 'Jim' to give her a tip on properties around Dallas. That lie had come so easily to him that he hadn't even considered trying to make it a reality until after he'd said it. Sometimes he kicked himself for the times he would say anything to make the conversation go his way. He had in mind his old acquaintance Benny. He'd met Benny in Dallas many years ago and wasn't sure where to find him now but he'd give that a shot in the morning. Jake didn't believe Ida was serious about properties anyway but he might as well play along and make the scam flow.

He had to walk quite a distance to his car from the restaurant as he'd made sure Ida wouldn't be able to watch him out a window to see what he was driving. The caprice was not a terrible car at all, in fact it was very comfortable, but it was not what the established or even the up and coming would be driving in most cases. If she saw that, she could be lost for good and he didn't want to take any chances. The evening was rather balmy so the walk was pleasurable and he took in that pleasure in spite of the noise of the hustle and bustle of the city. Being just a few blocks off the Dallas North Tollway there was plenty of noise, especially when a couple of crotch rockets went racing down that six lane. Jake could fancy himself riding one of those ultra quick rice grinders but had never purchased one as he was always on the move. He'd probably be a danger to himself and everyone else anyway; it was probably better he didn't.

The drive to the hotel was uneventful and Jake got himself ready for bed with musings of Ida on his mind. She really was an incredibly beautify woman and he had to wonder why she was still single and carousing about the single's scenes so long after her husband was gone. He was sure it was not for grieving; he couldn't see her being that attached to old man Periwinkle. He had been a source of income and all concerned knew it. Who could say? But his thoughts wandered to how nice it might be to wake up next to her every morning. That would be a mistake if he ever allowed it to happen, he would lose every bit of the freedom for which he'd always worked so hard. Although it would be nice to finally live in one place and not forever be covering his tracks, he had more of a tropical climate in his mind for his retirement. He so unprofessionally fell into slumber with imaginings of her naked body next to his.

CHAPTER THREE:
SETTING THE HOOK

The sun rose early this time of year and Jake still found himself awake and craving his morning cup of joe before the first rays came through the small opening he'd left in the curtains to ensure he'd get up. He walked to the office to use their coffee and creamers this morning, he was rich beyond anything he'd ever hoped as a child yet he still held to the habits he'd learned young from being poor. Always use what was given freely and keep your own to yourself. It wasn't selfish, he told himself, it was frugal and frugality had served him well. They had a few cheap cookies there on the same table with the coffee and Jake took just three because it rhymed with free. He recalled his childhood when his mother had taught him that little trick to keeping her weight in check, controlling one's appetite while not sacrificing one's sanity and obsessing over weight. In reality it was an obsession but it was a healthy obsession.

Today he had to find Benny, if that was possible; Benny the BS artist was a bit of a low life but he was still good people deep down in his heart and Jake felt he might count on him in a pinch. He used to hang out with him in Deep Ellum in his early days in Dallas and benny didn't seem like a guy that would change old habits. Originally called Deep Elm, as much of the activity centered around Elm Street just east of downtown Dallas, the pronunciation 'Deep Ellum' by early residents gave rise to the district's current name. A lot had been done to renovate the district in recent years and for all Jake knew, it may have become more highbrow than Benny would like. It was still an area for artisans and that meant poverty so it could still be the perfect stomping grounds for Benny. But Benny had a gift that made him one of a kind in a city, even one as big as this; he had a memory that never forgot anything. He called it a curse but he was amazing at times with what he knew. Jake was even rather jealous of that little Danny Devitto look alike.

Deep Ellum would be heavy with traffic already this morning being in the deepest part of down town and Jake needed to get on the stick if he wanted to get a parking space and then to find Benny. The only drawback with getting Benny to help would be that Benny, being a very intelligent type of guy, would want a piece of the action. But that was the price Jake would have to pay and if he could pull this off, it would be well worth the cost. The one thing Jake could always assure himself when he came to Dallas was the psychotic drivers that seemed to grace the town. What a pain in the arss!

He was not at all disappointed this time either. Before he had even gotten to his exit from Highway Seventy-Five, he'd had five near misses from the morons that frequented the roads around town. He was happy to take the exit to Live Oak Street, then a left on North Pearl Street and another left on Elm Street. Pretty simple to get there if one lived through it. It was already past eight a.m. when Jake finally parked near Terry Black's Barbeque; a relatively new place but one Jake knew about. At this point he'd be on foot trying to locate Benny and who knows, maybe they'd be enjoying some barbeque together for lunch. The morning was a bit warmer than he'd expected already and he peeled off his sweater that he'd needed that morning. He wrapped it around his waist and tied it off.

As he walked, jake realized he didn't really fit in with what he was wearing and it drew more attention than he wanted. It was too late now to go back to the room to change so he just continued even though he felt like a glaring spot light for an assault. If someone looked friendly, he'd stop and ask if they knew Benny and although a few said they'd heard of him, they had not seen him in months. Jake was beginning to worry Benny had moved on, but around eleven o'clock a homeless man approached him and said for five bucks he'd tell him where to find Benny. Jake went back and forth with the man because he suspected the old dude wasn't on the up and up but what was five bucks to him? In the end he gave the unshaven, dirty man a five-dollar bill in the hopes he wasn't pulling his leg. To his surprise, the old guy moved close like he had a secret to tell and with the nasty rotten tooth breath he said in a low voice, "He's on the DL living under the overpass at seventy-five and IH-thirty, He's in a drain pipe down there most of the time if it's not raining but he has a two-man pup tent nearby if it is raining. It's dark gray."

With that the informant turned and was gone into a nearby liquor store and Jake was left wondering how good the information was. At this point he had no choice but to take the man's word for it and bust a move over there on the surface streets. It wasn't more than ten or twelve minutes away and he could have walked it in twenty, but the sun was well up by that time and he had already broken a sweat. Besides, he could leave his sweater in the car now. He made his way back to his Caprice and rolling down the electric windows he fired up the air conditioner. He thought to himself, he'd gotten a pretty good deal on this old beast; everything worked. Soon the heat soak was gone from the car and he rolled the windows back up to keep the nice 50°F air from escaping. He was just beginning to dry out when he reached his destination and only had to find a break in the fence to access the area the old bum had described. He saw that break down in a gully not far from the described intersection of the highways and he found a place in the shade to park his car under one of the many viaducts.

Jake had almost missed the break in the fence because it was well down in the little gully and fairly well hidden from the road. As Jake walked down to the location, he found a slippery patch in the grass and found himself on his butt. That wasn't in the plan. Carefully making it the rest of the way down he found that someone had gathered tiny pieces of wire from something unknown and used several dozen to tie back the edges of the fence. Rather considerate of that person. At least he'd only have to launder his pants and not replace his shirt from a tear on the cut edges of the cyclone fencing.

Once inside the area of the drainage system it wasn't long before Jake spotted a gray tent near a four-foot diameter drainage culvert and made his way over there. He didn't find anyone, but there were signs of recent habitation so he decided to wait until the occupant made their way back; hopefully it was Benny. At least the area was shaded and well enough protected that the noise of the highways was almost relaxing. Jake almost fell asleep several times but he didn't dare do that in case the person that owned the camp site was not as friendly as Benny had always been. As small as he was, Benny had almost no choice but to be friendly. He certainly couldn't do anyone much damage and his sense of humor had gotten him out of more than a few scrapes.

Rather unexpectedly, Jake found himself startled awake by a gruff voice from behind his left ear, low and gravely, "What the hell do you think you're doing here?"
He popped up like a jack in the box and spun in one motion to face little Benny the BS'r!
Jake couldn't help himself but to pick up the little man in a bear hug and laugh at him, dirty and smelly as he was, he was a sight for sore eyes. Now he'd need to launder his shirt also. Benny, of course recognized Jake as he'd crawled out of the culvert and taken advantage of his friend's moment of sleep to sneak up on him. It may have been years but Benny couldn't forget anything and he and Jake had always been as close as two people of the

street might be.

When the moment presented itself, Benny turned toward the culvert and waved at the old guy that Jake had paid for the information. He waved back and was gone back into the culvert. "Ya, old Bob tracked me down and let me know you'd be here. I was just out getting some fresh food from the local restaurant garbage cans and he described you to a 'T'."

"Awe, Benny! If I'd known you were on hard times, I'd have come out here sooner!"

"I know you would have. But I had no idea how to get a hold of you. You change burner phones more than you do your own undershorts."

"Ya, I know. It's necessary. How come you're down here eating scraps? Did you lose everything?"

"Oh, HELL no! I'm not that stupid, you should know me, I've got plenty stashed back, I just can't get to it 'cause this new guy came to town and he's trying to kill me. I can barely get out to scrape up food sometimes."

"What kind of trouble did you get yourself into this time, Benny?"

"That's just it, I don't know. I find out one day this Lee Roy guy is gunning for me, something about snitching him out. One day someone does a drive by on me and I've got no idea where this is coming from, so I hightailed it down here and I've been hiding out ever since. I spend most of my time in the pipe over there in case someone might see me. It's been three months! Folks up top tell me he and his boys are still looking for me every single day."

"Damn! That's rough Benny."

"Tell me about it! It's worse than being in jail."

"I tell you what, Benny. Let's pack you out of here right now. My car isn't far up the road and I've got a room at the motel six. I'll just let them know I'm changing it up to double occupancy."

"You'd do that for me, Jake?"

"Well, ya! I know you'd help me out in a pinch!"

"Maybe; I'm just playing with you."

"I know you are, Benny."

Benny was already tearing down his tent and gathering up his meager belongings. Jake didn't have to say it twice and Benny was johnny on the spot.

"By the way, I need your help too. Just so you know, your name is Jim and I'm Charles Gordon."

"What, I've got no last name?"

"I didn't have time so you get to pick your own."

"My last name is always Benny in these cases. That way if you mess up it sounds natural."

"Oh, I like that, Jim Benny. Good idea."

"Ya, right?"

"So, tell me the scam."

They carried Benny's goods up the hill while Jake was giving him the scoop on the gorgeous mark. Benny was all ears especially when Jake was describing what Ida had been wearing when they first met. He was quite impressed at Jake's choice of victim and curious why he hadn't tried to close the deal, as he put it, that first night.

"Oh, no Benny, this woman is too smart and thinks too highly of herself for that. I didn't want to blow the whole deal just for a piece of tail."

"Ya, I guess you're right. It's been so long since I've had any, that I'd have offered to dive on her muff right there and then."

Jake laughed a loud guffa. "I can understand that little guy, but this may work best with extreme patience and just let her make the first move."

"Okay, okay," Benny agreed. "It sounds like you have her all scoped out."

"I don't know about that, but I'm thinking that she's like most women and want's it, but she'll need to trust me first and that could take some doing."

"Right."

They'd made it to Jake's car and the first thing out of Benny's mouth was, "Where'd you find this piece of shit?"

"Awe, come on Benny, it ain't so bad. The windows, A.C. and

radio work."

"All right, but you'll never snag her in this thing."

"I wasn't planning on it. I'll see what I can do about getting a handle on a C320."

"A C320? So, you're not filthy rich in this scam?"

"No, but it's still a Mercedes and if I get something that's fairly new, that will bode well."

"Ya, I can see that. It should work. You know, if you want me to be a respectable property broker I'll need a suit. I haven't had one in years. Are you okay with doing that for me?"

"Of course, Benny, you just do your homework and I'll take good care of you."

"Okay, ten percent and the suit?"

"you're worth every penny of it."

"Ya, I am, aren't I?"

They both laughed because they knew Benny was right. He was worth it. Jake was happy to have found him and Benny was giving him a huge break at ten percent.

"But first a bath, shave and a haircut for you, old friend."

Jake was breaking one of his cardinal rules by bringing Benny in on this, but he needed him and they both knew it.

* * *

That night they opted to stay out of sight this close to Deep Ellum and ordered in a pizza while Benny used Jakes laptop to locate some properties; after a shower of course. The haircut and shave would come in the morning. First some properties for Jake to pretend to look at and then a couple for Ida. Benny wasn't sure what her tastes were so he looked for some apartments, a couple of fourplex's and he found an upscale home near Ipswich that was only moderately overpriced. Ipswich had a very small but nice area before it was downgraded, further on, by businesses. But having local places for shopping and eating made it a good all-around choice. He found a few others for her in the same area where he planned to put Jake's interests. What he found for Jake was on the West side of Preston North of the PGBTP (President George Bush Turn Pike).

The next day was a Sunday so they started early with the shave and haircut and then went driving around looking at what Benny had found. Benny about wanted to knock Jake out when Jake offered to get him a booster seat for the drive but it was all in fun. This was serious business if they wanted to make the right impression on Ida and they both were doing their best to find just the right properties. They spent most of the day out looking but by four in the afternoon they'd found what they wanted to show Ida and knew what they'd show to her if she asked to see what Jake Sullivan... Charles Gordon was considering. They stopped off on the Dallas North Tollway, again at the shops at Legacy and found a little eatery to have a bite of dinner. Jake figured there was little chance Lee Roy would be looking for Benny all the way North like this. It was a nice little hole in the wall and was actually quite small and cozy for that area. The fare was very well prepared and the presentation was phenomenal. By the time they left, Benny was claiming he wanted to buy the place. Jake just laughed at him as he knew that wasn't going to happen.

The next order of business was a suit for Benny. It couldn't be some piece of garbage off the rack or even an upscale chain store it had to be the real deal because Ida would know the difference. It would cost jake a ton for this but if Benny pulled off his part, it would make life a lot easier for Jake. Jake wanted to make things as real as possible so he and Benny set about finding him a supposed relative that had died last Thursday morning back in Shreveport so that he could drive back there and grieve for a few days. This would create enough doubt in Ida's mind that when 'Charles' showed back up with Jim Benny, it would look good as gold. They set about getting Benny some business cards and a counterfeit agent license in case Ida checked. She wouldn't likely, but why chance it? By the time they were done that night at eleven thirty, Jim Benny was a Bonafede broker and they had their game faces on.

Jake called Ida the next day from his burner phone and let her know the bad news about his great Aunt Nōna; the last relative he had from his mother's side of the family. In the conversation he let her know he'd contacted Jim Benny and that Jim had already located some properties she might like.

"Oh, really, Charles? Did he happen to say what area?"

Jake thought that was said with a touch of sarcasm, as though there might be some disbelief.

"Yes, he said one was near Ipswich and there were a few North of the PGBT off of Preston."

"Those areas are great for resale; I wonder how they are priced?"

"Jim didn't elude to anything on the properties North of the PGBT but he said the one near Ipswich was not terribly overpriced, his words, not mine. I'm assuming one could make an offer and they should likely consider it as it's been on the market for a year now."

"That sounds like it could hold promise. I'm truly sorry about your aunt, do you have any idea when you'll be back?"

"I'm not sure, but The Funeral is set for this Thursday and I'm hoping I'll be back late Friday or Early Saturday."

"That's an odd day for a funeral. Well then, I look forward to hearing from you when you arrive back. I'd tell you to enjoy your trip but I'm sure that would be less than appropriate."

"It will be good to see the extend family regardless of the circumstances, that's always a nice time even though it won't be a standard family gathering."

"Okay, well, you be careful and be sure to call when you get back, Charles."

"Of course, I look forward to seeing you again also, Ida."

Jake was pleased with how the call went. It was obvious that Ida didn't fully believe him but she was still open to the possibility he might be telling the truth. Benny had found the perfect death announcement from which they could make a document to prove he was there. Nōna was such a common name in the south as it wasn't really a name but a reference to an older grandmotherly woman. The announcement gave her name as Patricia Cherry Gordon 'known as Nōna to her friends and relatives', it had a photo and she had no surviving children which was beyond hope for a scam like this. Jake wouldn't have to lie about their relationship as he had always used his mother's last name, Sullivan in truth, but it fit right in with the story. Well, it was a lie but not a lie, sort of. The fewer lies the less he had to keep track of. That's why Benny was so great at this, he never forgot anything. Benny made a file on a thumb drive and they went to that office place just up the street to make a document for 'Charles' to bring back from Shreveport.

The technician behind the counter told them it was five dollars to do the job even if it was only one sheet because of the set-up time. Benny about went over the counter to teach that snot nosed kid a lesson but sufficed to tell him there was no set up time involved. Plug in the thumb drive and print! And the kid then told him it was company policy. Benny wanted blood. But that was Benny, he watched every cent and didn't let anyone take him to the cleaners. In the end they paid the five dollars and left with Benny grumbling the entire way. Jake could only laugh at him and that infuriated Benny even more.
"They get you coming and going! That's why I don't mind doing what we do. Everyone is scamming somehow some way and they all get their pound of flesh, why shouldn't we?"
"I know Benny, it's a dog-eat-dog world and that's why we have to keep our heads low and run in the middle of the pack. That way no one suspects us of being the big dogs and they don't challenge us."
"I suppose you're right," said Benny, "It still frosts my balls and it gets old."
Jake could only laugh.

While Charles was away in Shreveport, Jake and Benny had nothing to do but sit idle in the room and watch old movies on cable TV and play cards. They still needed to get a suit for Benny but that had to be done by appointment only where they were going. This motel Six didn't have a swimming pool as the real estate was too expensive in down town. The city made too much money on it in taxes as well. That's why many of the cheap motels had moved out of the area and the ones that stayed weren't so cheap anymore. Even the prostitutes had to jack up their prices to use the rooms. Jake didn't know that from experience but the young man behind the night desk gave them all of the details and greeted the girls by name as they came in to rent by the night. Apparently, few of them used the same location two nights in a row but they made a circuit through the available places that wouldn't rat them out to the po-po. They eventually became friendly to the night clerks as sooner or later they were recognizable as regular customers. And Jake had to admit, there were some that were very recognizable in a big town like this. There was no lack of talent and many of them used their profits to dress at the best clothiers around town. Jake could imagine some of them getting a bit better price at the Marriot or someplace that had an upscale restaurant and bar. Possibly at the airport.

It was just a waiting game at this point and because Benny was a wanted man and he was certain Lee Roy had people that would recognize him they stayed in mostly. He still maintained that he had no idea how Lee Roy had come to the conclusion that he'd snitched on him. Benny didn't know the guy until just before he'd tried to kill him one night in a drive by. That was an advantage of being a small target.
"Maybe it was someone else that snitched on him?" Jake asked.
"Maybe, I don't know who. You know me, I don't make enemies, except maybe counter clerks overcharging for copies." They both laughed a bit at Benny's little tirade earlier that day.

"Best I can figure, Jake, is like you say, that someone else wants me dead for whatever reason and snitched on Lee Roy and blamed it on me."

"But who would do that to you?"

"You've got me. I can't think of anyone. You know I don't shit where I eat so I can't think of anyone here locally. I just might have to clear out of this town. Maybe go to Houston or Auston for a while."

"How much money do you have stashed, Benny? Not an exact figure..." Jake knew Benny would never tell him the exact number, "is it enough to retire yet?"

"Hmmm, maybe. You know I won't tell you how much, but I'm getting close."

"I've got an idea. What if this job were to pay what you need to call it quits? I'm close too, maybe Aruba or Montego. What do you think?"

"Could you go for Costa Rica?"

"Now you're talking!"

Jake wasn't sure if Benny was serious, about retiring together but it was not out of the realm of reality for him. Jake had never had a partner but he knew he had a friend in Benny and with him, it might just work out.

"Did you get that appointment for your suit?"

"You know I'd never forget a detail like that. Ya, this afternoon at three, Over a bit East of here near the Galleria."

"What did they say about a time frame to get it tailored?"

"Sorry, Jake, but money talks, it's going to be an extra Two-Hundred-fifty."

"Ouch! You'd better be worth it!"

"Ya, I know, right? I've got my ducks in a row. It's all about how she responds, and that's where your silver tongue comes in."

"We can do this."

They made their way to the clothier Benny had found and it was a right nice place that served drinks while one waited. Probably to loosen up cash clips and wallets of the show-off trust fund babies. Some younger salesman pounced on them right away and had the server bring them something with an umbrella in it. Jake didn't catch the name of it but it was plenty good tasting. Benny immediately went to the rack with Brioni hanging and found a subtly dark gray pinstripe in his waist and jacket size. The gentleman helping him was truly terrible at hiding his amusement at Benny's size and Benny just about had a melt down on the guy.

"What the f*** is your problem, d*** wad?"

Jake nearly busted a gut laughing and benny gave him a look of death, "I'm going to remember in Costa Rica that you laughed."

"I truly apologize, sir. We seldom get anyone of your stature and it was a bit of a shock for me. Shall I get someone else to help you?"

"Ya, make it the owner, I want to complain about you while I wait."

"Certainly sir."

A moment later an older gentleman approached that apologized and asked if he could be of assistance.

Benny didn't hesitate, "Ya, fire that other dip shit."

"He will be dealt with sir."

"I'll just bet."

"I like this Brioni, can you tailor it to fit me by Friday?"

"Sir, that is a fine piece of clothing but we have several others in front of yours. It generally takes two weeks to alter a suit."

"One of your associates told me over the phone it would be Two-Hundred-fifty to have it by Friday. Was he lying?"

"Well, sir. That is a tall order but we can try."

The tall order slight was not wasted on Benny.

"For fifty-five-hundred and an extra two-fifty you can try pretty damned hard."

"Yes, sir."

"Get someone over here to fit it to me."

"Of course, sir. Very good, sir"

It was almost an hour as the tailor took Benny's measurements. All the while shaking his head as if wondering how he'd accomplish this. Jake had already slipped Benny the cash after seeing the price so when the total was presented by the owner, Benny took great joy.

"That will be four-thousand-seven-hundred-fifty dollars sir. Will that be charge or debit?"

"How about cash, punk?"

It pleased both Benny and Jake when the owner was taken back a bit by Benny's response.

"Joseph, could you bring the bill counter from the back, please?"

A young man showed up and placed the counting machine on the register counter and plugged it in to a floor plug. Benny handed the man a stack and the machine counted out four-thousand-eight-hundred dollars.

"I'll get your change sir."

"Damned right you'll get my change, and don't expect a tip; punk"

What would the supposed owner do? Hit a man that stood only four feet eleven inches, one inch too tall to be considered a midget?

As the two walked out the front door and headed for the Caprice, again innocuously parked away from sight, Jake laughed and said, "Man, it would have been so much easier to just punch him in the face!"

"Ya, but it wouldn't have been as much fun! And I can't reach up that high."

"No, doubt!"

They both had a good laugh and wondered what the conversation was back at the clothier shop.

They were ready for some dinner at this point and Pappadeaux was nearby and not a bad price. The lobster was tempting sitting in an aquarium as they walked in the front door but Jake had his heart set on fresh oysters and an alligator steak while Benny went ahead and had the lobster and a mini fillet medium rare. Jake ordered a dozen oysters so he could share them with Benny and they had a good conversation concerning the day's escapades, where to rent a Mercedes for Saturday and where they might live in Costa Rica. Pappadeaux was always busy especially with the influx of folks displaced by hurricane Katrina. It had been over a decade and many simply didn't want to go back to Louisiana to rebuild. They had found it comfortable here in Dallas, the pay was comparable and often better in their chosen fields and there was no state income tax. They had no reason to go back.

Tomorrow, they had to get their rental car set up for Saturday morning. Especially as Jake had no credit card for the rental company to hold. They had waited maybe a little longer than they should have to get it done but Benny knew a guy that knew a guy and was sure he could get it arranged. 'Charles' would call Ida Thursday evening and let her know the plan was for him to drive back Friday morning and that the arrangements had been made to tour the properties on Saturday morning. If she saw something she liked, Jim Benny could call the listing broker to make the arrangement to see it up close and personal.

"Why don't we meet at Arthur's Friday night for dinner," Ida asked.

"I was not expecting that and already made arrangements with Jim. Would you mind if I brought Jim with me and we can make it a threesome, for dinner I mean, of course." Ida caught the off-color joke and snickered more to be polite than anything else. "That way you can meet him and we can all get to know each other."

"That would be wonderful!" exclaimed Ida. I would love to meet your friend."

"I'm so glad you feel that way. I've known Jim for years and although we don't get together as much as either of us would like, he's kind of an integral part of my life."

"Of course, by all means! I'd love to hear stories about your younger years from his point of view."

Umm, no she wouldn't, but Jake was sure that Jim Benny could come up with something appropriate for himself and Charles.

Jake suspected Ida was either being extremely polite or she was being extremely careful in ferreting out the truth about Charles Gordon and Jim Benny.

"Then it's a date! I'm so looking forward to this! Thanks for making all the arrangements!"

"It's my pleasure, Ida. This seems to be a meeting of the minds through coincidence and I'm just amazed at how it's working so well for us both. By the way, is seven thirty too early?"

"Seven thirty would be just fine."

Jake made a pass at Ida that could be blown off as a neutral compliment but it was very well received and he knew she was beginning to believe his story. They said their goodbyes and the plan was finally in motion.

Benny decided to see if his friend of a friend could get the C320 for Friday afternoon and got on the hotel phone before Jake had even said his goodbyes to Ida. They didn't get the call back until one a.m. but the arrangements had been made. Somebody was making too much money on the deal. It was Five hundred up front, five grand deposit and a first-born child if there was damage. But beggars can't be choosers and both Jake and Benny approved the deal. They would pick up the car on Friday at Noon and have it back by Sunday at noon. Not much different from a rental company but on the down low. Jake figured the guy that knew a guy actually worked for a rental company or something and this was a brand-new vehicle. He would not be disappointed. As it turned out, the car came from the local Mercedes dealership in North Plano on highway 75 and when they picked it up from Jake's friend it was clean as a whistle and looking like down town! Benny had come through one more time. They scraped off the decals that identified it as a rental or whatever it was, when they returned it, what would the dealership say? Wanna be big shots did that stuff all the time and they were no different, the dealership would just put more stickers on the car. Oddly, it had permanent plates instead of dealer plates but Jake/Charles wasn't sure that was an issue, Jim Benny agreed.

Charles decided to dress a bit better for their Friday night date with Ida. No Five-thousand-dollar suit like Benny but he would sport a beige leather jacket, gray silk shirt, black wool slacks and a silk tie. Benny called the clothier and made sure the suit would be ready on Friday which they assured him it would. They showed up at nine a.m. just as the supposed owner opened the doors. He was a bit more congenial today as it was quite obvious that Jim Benny was a man of means that they had not suspected; albeit new money, from his apparent attitude. That was one thing Benny had, it was attitude. That was why Jake/Charles knew he could always count on Jim Benny. After picking up the suit, they both got fresh haircuts and made all the necessary arrangements for the personal attire accoutrements required for a lady of style and class like Ida. Jake still saw her as the mark but Charles was beginning to like Ida. Jim Benny hoped that wouldn't be a problem.

The boys arrived at Arthur's a bit early to ensure they'd get a good table and both ordered a drink to give them something to do while waiting on Ida. It would be good for them both to relax with a little alcohol because this would make or break the situation. Too much alcohol, of course, would kill the deal so they would be careful. They didn't have to wait too long as Ida was apparently a punctual person and was there at seven thirty-two according to Charles' watch. He appreciated a woman that could be on time. That was a rare find all by itself. Not to disparage women of course, but it was true.

"Welcome, welcome," was Charles' opening remark. "You look even more stunning tonight! This is Jim Benny."

"It's a true pleasure to make your acquaintance, Mrs. Periwinkle," with all the charm he could muster. It wasn't difficult to be charming toward this woman because she was everything Jake had said she was.

"Please, Mr. Benny, call me Ida."

"Of course, and please call me Mr. Benny... that's a joke of course.

I'd love for you to call me Jim, simply Benny would work in a pinch as well."

"Of course, simply Benny."

"Charles, you didn't tell me Ida had jokes. She's quick on the uptake."

"She does seem to have a quick wit and that denotes intellect as well," Jim putting on as much charm as he could as well.

"Not to be too formal but please allow me to give you my card, Ida."

"Thank you, Jim." Ida slipped it into her black hand bag. Benny wondering if she would check out his credentials. He'd made a very small but professional web page in addition to everything else. So, she could check him out all she wanted and Benny felt there would be no question as to his validity. She'd already noted the Brioni tailor fit suit as she sized him up (so to speak) upon entering. That in itself would go a long way in establishing Jim Benny as being legit. Right away Ida was asking Benny about the early days of his and Charle's relationship; this woman didn't slow down in legitimizing who they were. She was not a novice at determining who people were.

"I heard Charles talking of his need to start investing at a bar one night about 15 years ago…"

"Oh, you two have known each other for a while then?"

"For just a minute or two."

"That was The Mansion Bar, wasn't it, Jim?"

"That's as I recall."

"Jim, has a memory that never forgets anything. If he learns it, he's better that an encyclopedia."

"That must be extremely useful, Jim."

"Ya, but it's also a curse because it's too easy to hold a grudge, So, don't upset me." He said with a smile. "Still, it's a good curse," He continued.

"I can only imagine."

The server had been busy in the back with something but came over and apologized for being slow and gave them all menus. He took their drink orders and came back with them to take their dinner orders. It only took Ida a moment as she obviously knew the menu well, belying her habit of frequenting the place.

Benny and Charles took a few moments but everything on the menu looked good. They made their orders and the conversation continued until their food arrived. After a few bights they continued to get to know each other and Benny proved his ability at conversing and keeping Ida at bay concerning her prying into their past. He gave her just enough to satiate her curiosity while not revealing much of anything but generalities.

Charles held up his part of the conversation as well speaking of his Great Aunt Nōna and the gathering of relations from across the country. He used the names and locations of his real relations so he wouldn't forget. Ida spoke of old man Periwinkle and how they'd met and married. His children's guarded acceptance of her and his final days; she never once mentioned money which was likely a very practiced behavior. Regardless of what anyone thinks, there are just as many men looking to marry for money as there are women. And the methods are very similar across the board.

When they were done Charles was a bit surprised when Ida announced she'd like to head home and be up early for their tour of the properties. But he made no hesitation in accepting that idea and dinner was essentially over in a flash. Benny mentioned it had been rather anticlimactic when they were alone and Charles had to agree. But that was not a bad idea for Ida to set forth and they couldn't argue without seeming rude or manipulative. Maybe that's what she was trying to feel out in this game of three-D chess. They would pick Ida up at her home at nine o'clock in the morning and the game would continue.

CHAPTER FOUR: THE MAGICAL MYSTERY TOUR

It was nice to climb into the smell of new leather seats that enveloped him and start the quiet 3.2-liter motor that one barely noticed running. It was far different from the ten-year old Caprice. The Caprice was a good solid car but this was a driving machine. It was far too expensive a car for what it offered but reasonable next to many of the US luxury cars. Those that had their sites set high in the world would recognize this low-end model as belonging someone ready to move up as appearances could make or break deals. It was perfect for this scenario and Ida would recognize all it meant being chauffeured around by Charles and Jim to see these properties.

Charles and Jim were early to arrive at Ida's but that would be a faux pas. So, they parked down the road a bit and waited until exactly nine a.m. to drive up her circular drive and park at the front door. The house was far larger in the back than the front but its size was well represented regardless. It was also quite ornate in the large, almost gaudy trim around the windows and front double forty-inch entry doors. The entry gate to the drive had apparently been left open in expectation of their arrival. Ida was at the front door opening it to them immediately as though she saw them coming, Charles and Jim both took note of the security camera above their heads; and the one inside the door. "Gentlemen, would you like the grand tour?"

There was no hesitation from Jim, "Absolutely!"
And Charles just smiled and nodded in affirmation.

It was a gorgeous older house, possibly a hundred years old but well updated for the day and sporting lightly stained wood trim work, mop boards and crown moldings that were ornate and overly large bespeaking of the wealth of the person that had it built. Chandeliers in every room except the library that had only one two bulb ceiling lamp in the center of the ceiling and several reading lamps around the perimeter each one over a chair or a small sitting table. One might expect that arrangement in a library. It also had book shelves lining most of three walls all the way to the twelve-foot ceiling that were filled with new and old books. All the floors were of highly polished oak with woven wool area carpets in every room and runners in the halls to protect the floors.

The French doors at the back of the house revealed a large Koi-pond with a Seven-foot fountain bubbling down four tears of ever larger pools in the center. Well-kept gardens with finely trimmed grass paths running between were pristine and sharp edged. It was a piece of art and both Benny and Charles made that quite plain. There was a covered, exposed aggregate porch with black painted cast iron furniture of a flower pattern. Not overly expensive for a back porch but a very nice touch and the Koi-pond butted up to its edge.

After sufficient oohing and ahing Ida led the boys back to the front door and suggested getting their morning's tour started. After Ida set the alarm and locked up, Jim went for the rear door of the C320 and Charles walked Ida to the front passenger seat and opened the door for her. Ida knew her place in this group and showed no surprise but uttered a congenial, "Thank you," for the courtesy. Before Charles had made his way to the driver's seat Ida had found the funeral leaflet folded lengthwise and conveniently left in the phone holder in the dash. She had no inkling of privacy of something left out in the open and had already unfolded it and started reading through it.

It seemed strange to her that Charles had failed to remove it from the car... Another piece of the plot put into the picture of the puzzle. There was no longer any reason for Ida to question their sincerity. Ida obviously enjoyed the leather interior as her fingers traced the stitching of the seat, a small smile played on her lips. As they drove off to view the properties, the car glided through the streets, a silent testament to their aspirations. The Caprice, with its solid build and years of service, was reliable but would have to be left behind when this caper was finished.

They drove first to the property at Ipswich for Ida's sake and found the house easily enough. Benny mentioned there was an upscale fourplex just up the road if she cared to drive by there as well and she was open to the idea. They sat in front of the house for a few minutes as Jim rattled off the home's amenities from memory. Ida was duly impressed at his memory and Jim turned a shade of red at her praise although she didn't notice with him in the back seat. But Gordon could see quite well in the rear-view mirror and smiled at Benny a knowing smile that only friends would communicate. One could tell he had not been around too many women of her stunning good looks and that was not wasted on Ida, she seemed to take notice of everything. Only a block away was the fourplex and it was indeed upscale, a very nice arrangement with a garage and carport for each unit, well-trimmed bushes and shade trees that encompassed the property. One almost didn't suspect it to be a multiple family dwelling by the landscaping but for the repetitive front windows and doors. Ida liked both of the properties and wanted to tour them both. She certainly seemed to be looking to improve her net worth through property ownership.

They moved on to the properties North of the PGBT and many of these were very high end many being in the multiple millions of dollars. Charles turned down flat those that were over a million but showed interest in those just above a half million. Except for the small eight-unit apartment building out near Preston. That wasn't in his price range but he said he could make it work if the bank could make it work. That seemed to please Ida. An entrepreneur had to be willing to take risks if they were to get ahead and a move on this type of property could lead to much bigger and better things. Jake was almost convincing himself he should actually make this move. He'd actually be legitimate. Having money is a good thing but having money make money for you, is even better. He might have to give it some serious thought. Benny saw the wheels turning in Jakes head and was worried he might have to talk him down. But then again, Jake was a big boy and could take care of himself. Benny figured Jake could bear some watching over.

They had missed lunch but it was a very productive morning and Ida was caught up in the moment. They decided to stop at a Braum's ice cream and they drew all kinds of attention, Jim in his Brioni Suit, Gordon and Ida in their upscale attire pulling up in a Mercedes C320. What a sight to see but in all honesty, Ida had to agree that Braum's had some of the best ice cream in the world. They sat there in all their spectacle and enjoyed their afternoon treat.
"What do you think, Jim?" Ida seemed to be bringing Benny into a position of full trust in her mind.
"Let me get a hold of the listing brokers and I'll let you know tomorrow. That's all we can really do at this point. The ones you like would be my choices as well, they have great curb appeal, good locations and the prices are already right; I made sure of that before dragging you all the way out here."
Benny was being cautious as well as encouraging which was his only play until he could set up actual walk throughs. In high end, properties like these the listing broker might want to be along for the purpose of giving their own rundown to help make the sale. So often the listing agents on places didn't really care and they would just provide a lock box code to obtain a key but

none of these had that in the listing information. He'd make the calls this evening and maybe they could look around inside tomorrow. Charles and Jim dropped Ida off at her place and went back to their motel room.

Once Ida was out of the car the real planning began as they'd gotten to see exactly what they had needed when Ida gave them the tour of her house; but for one thing... where was the safe with the cash?
"She's just got a standard alarm system like anyone else."
"Did you see where the DVR for the cameras is located? Benny, we need that info."
"I know, I know. Maybe we can ferret that from her tomorrow; I'm just not sure how we should approach it."
"How do you want to disable the alarm? I didn't see phone lines; it looks like a cell-based unit."
"Ya, a standard jammer should work on that."
"Did you see the quality of those cameras, though? Those could find a flea on a dog's back at a hundred yards, Benny."
"Ya, in color even and most of them mounted so far up we can't reach them to disable them."
"Well, you can't reach them, anyway."
Benny tried to chase Jake into the room but it was no contest; he just acted out his hurt feelings until Jake let him take a faux swing and a miss at him.
"You want to take bets the safe is in the floor somewhere? I saw a door off the bedroom she didn't open for us, like a safe room. A safe in a safe room, maybe?"
"That wouldn't be in the floor then, Jake. I hate to suggest it 'cause I already know you'll get all tangled up in her, but you want to try and bed her for the information?"
"Well, sure I want to, who wouldn't? But I don't think we're at that point yet. Let's just assume that's where it is for now; probably the DVR for the cameras too."
"Ya, it would make sense. Did you notice wires on the cameras?"
"I sure did. Line of sight RF cameras don't work well on these

brick facade Texas houses."

"Good, that means we might be able to chase the wires with a stud finder if we need to. We can rent one at that home improvement place just up the road from her house just in case we need it. I would go to the city for blue prints but that would leave a trail for the cops. Besides, that place is old money and that may not be on the prints." Benny was right. It wasn't likely that an alarm system or cameras would be on any prints. The house appeared to be at least fifty years old and there was an old guard shack on the grounds outside the gate. It was well kept but seemed more of a sign of older times than something that might actually be put to use.

"Jake, did you notice that man gate at the back of the yard?"

"Ya, I'm wondering where that goes myself. It looks like a good way in and those French-doors in back wouldn't stop any one without the alarm system."

"That's what I'm thinking. Easy in and easy out. We need to find out where that goes. Google Earth?"

"Google Earth."

A lot of times, general technology is not as good as it needs to be but Google Earth was originally started using CIA satellites and quite often had some of the best overhead photos available. Benny put in Ida's address and they had what they needed on screen in a matter of thirty seconds including the time to boot the laptop. Like so many places in Texas, neighborhoods, even old ones like Ida's, had alleys running between the properties for garbage disposal and garbage trucks. And that's just where the gate led. A one lane alleyway where polly garbage bins could be rolled out for pickup. Neither of them had previously noted the small fenced area at the back of the yard where the bins were kept hidden from view but they were clearly seen on Google Earth with a small concrete walkway to take them out to the alley.

That was the way into Ida's back yard. They were both betting there was no camera that far from the house to record activities back there. All the cameras Jake and Benny had noted were mounted directly to the house structure. But there were plenty of those and they were betting they were on motion sensing settings that would notify Ida by cell phone if not the local police as well. But even motion sensing cameras could be beaten. They would need a wireless jamming device for the internet service.

After all things were considered, Benny looked Jake in the eyes and asked, "Why don't we just cut the power to the place?"
"Well, what if her systems have battery back up?"
"We should be able to tell by the infrared lights in the cameras. We'll take the jammer with us just in case"
"That means we need a pair of binoculars as well to check out the ones in the back yard."
"Not really," said Benny. "The electric meter is on the side of the house where the electric lines go in. We'll need to get to that to cut power. We need to jam the wireless until we get that done. But that's a lot easier than any other plan we've had."
"Okay," said Jake. "So, in order of importance...
Jam the internet,
Pick the lock on the back gate,
Pull the electric meter,
Check the infrared camera lights,
Get into the French doors,
Disable any battery backup on the internet
Upstairs to the safe room,
Then we can complete the job."
"Right! We'll need to set the jammer up in the front of the house because the back gate is too far away. That means driving around to the back gate afterward. We need to scope out a place to park out back."
Once they cut the power, the battery backup that comes with almost all alarm systems would kick in. Most alarm systems let the owner know about it by email. But with the internet jammed, it should not be an issue; and they had not noticed Ida

being tied to her phone anyway. Then they'd only need to worry about a battery on the internet router. The jammer should be able to give them time to pull the alarm off the wall and disable it, they should be able to set that up in the guard shack outside the front gate. There had been a light on in there when they dropped Ida off the other evening so they knew there was power available. The plan was coming together.

They'd noted three cameras in the back yard and one of those might have been intended for the back gate if memory served them right. When they pulled this job, they'd have to locate the DVR and steal that as well just to be safe. They were fairly certain it would be in the same area as the safe. Jake made the phone calls to set up times to see the properties in which they were interested.

Tomorrow would be a big day for the three of them but it would be the icing on the cake for gaining Ida's trust. Benny emailed Ida the schedule for tomorrow and then texted her to let her know he'd sent the email. She responded to the text and the boys knew they were on for the morning. They would not be starting too early as so many agents were not too terribly anxious to get up before the sun; their first appointment being ten a.m. at the Ipswich house. That looked like a probable for Ida anyway and it would be a good gauge for the other places as far as bang for the buck. The properties at this point had become moot for Jake as Benny had talked long and hard to him about keeping his cash liquid for a bit longer. His reasoning was that if he really did invest, it was a means by which the police could track him and it would be best to wait for another opportunity. It made sense to Jake; he didn't want even a thread for the cops to pull on and unravel his entire life.

The morning wasn't even brisk for this time of year and Benny knew he'd need to launder his suit after this outing; least ways the shirt and vest. Ida was looking incredible in a low cut, mid-calf all-white sun dress with red bars over each shoulder, a red satin belt and red and white pumps. That outfit did not come from Wally World. These agents must be motivated to give appointments on a Sunday and the three of them agreed it might be because these units had all been on the market for a while. It made one wonder why as the prices were all fairly good but then again, they were on the upper end of the scale where there would be fewer buyers. As they met for each of the appointments nothing seemed obviously off about any of the units although the fourplex had not been cleaned up. It would require new carpets and paint but the right contractor would have that work done in a week and they could be rented out. The house on Ipswich was older but very well kept and Ida liked it a lot. But Benny and Jake could both see she was leaning toward the fourplex if Charles didn't jump on it. The nice thing about multiple family units is that when someone moved out, the income did not drop off completely.

As the sun began its descent, painting the sky in hues of orange and pink, fatigue weighed heavily on the group. They were about to leave when the agent, tasked with showing the eight-unit apartment building, arrived unfashionably late. Charles, was not impressed with the late arrival and barely masked his consternation and a smidge of malice. The empty unit before them stood silent, a hollow promise of possibilities. He feigned enthusiasm, though Jim's earlier caution about avoiding any trace that might attract the authorities' attention echoed in his mind. The po-po were not to be trifled with, and Charles played his part well, the very picture of a potential buyer. Ida, on the other hand, had been utterly charmed by the quaint allure of the fourplex. In a display of chivalry, Charles deferred to her preference, pretending to set aside his own ambitions for that property and pretending to like the idea of the eight unit place at which they were now looking. He could not leave behind a thread by which to trace him so it would be easy to fail to finance the larger place.

Jim Benny, ever the pragmatist, offered to gather estimates for the necessary renovations. His voice carried the weight of experience as he spoke of crafting a proposal for Ida to consider, an offer that might just turn her dreams into reality. Ida's heart fluttered with the prospect, yet she remained the epitome of composure. She had other investments but this was the first time she had considered property on a larger scale. Her excitement was a river running deep, its currents hidden beneath a serene surface. She assured Jim of her intent to pursue the fourplex, her eyes seeking Gordon's for confirmation. Gordon, with a flourish of gallantry, declared, "It's all yours, my lady," his voice melodious and rich with sincerity.

As twilight embraced the city, they bid farewell to Ida at her home. Promises were exchanged under the watchful eye of the fading day. Gordon and Jim vowed to reach out to Ida within the week; Jim with a proposal etched in numbers and practicality, and Gordon just to exchange starry eyed musings. As they departed, the guard shack beckoned for a cursory inspection. Jim's keen eyes spotted an outlet, low on one wall; likely for an electric heater during the chill of winter. Above, a 220V outlet perched, awaiting the hum of an AC unit in the heat of summer.

It seemed so odd to Jake that anyone would be so humbled as to work for Twelve dollars an hour and sometimes less to sit in a shack all day bored out their mind. But he supposed that in times of desperation one did as one must to keep the family fed. With the number of Illegals living in Dallas at this point, hoping for a better life, that might seem to be a gift from heaven. He had never been in that position but despite her many faults his mother had always insisted that Jake treat everyone with the same compassion and respect with which he would hope to be treated. He really did miss her at times and this evening the lessons she'd taught him, brought a tear to his eye.

Both Jake and Benny were exhausted by the tempo of the day and the ride back to the hotel was quite subdued. It was not long before Jake turned on the headlights and turned on the radio down low with the local country station playing cry in your beer songs. Benny changed that up real fast to some upbeat hip hop, real toe tapping stuff to lighten the mood and the volume came up dramatically. Jake could only smile because it really did coax their tired spirits back from the dead. They would have to return the C320 in the morning before noon and that was not a happy thought as it really was a very nice vehicle. But they were already a day over on the rental and that would cost them money on which they had not planned.

Jake had to ask, "Benny, what if we need this again next weekend, do you think we can get the same one?"
"I'm not sure, I can ask. I suppose it all depends on what part of inventory it came from and if they have enough to spare next week. Remember, we didn't see any rental stickers on it, it might be something the service department loans out. Especially with that permanent plate on it"
Jake thought that was a really good guess on Benny's part, that little guy was smarter than he looked. He had always impressed Jake with his ever-galloping thoughts and plans. He wondered how the little guy could sleep at night with all that going on up there. In spite of his diminutive stature, Benny was one hell of a brainiac and Jake respected him immensely on that count.

They set no alarms for the morning and didn't even leave the curtains apart to let the sun in. They might not have worked physically hard on Sunday but the mental strain of acting their roles did take its toll and it was not easy on them. To be especially sure of no disturbance they left the phone on, 'Do Not Disturb' with the office. Jake had already paid another weak in advance so there was no reason for the office to be so rude but one never knew in these situations. They ordered out a pizza tonight again and had stopped at the liquor store for some refreshments as well. In this part of town there was a liquor store about every mile or so because a lot of people were on foot. But that was not meant to be, much to their surprise.

Texas had dry counties and Dallas did not allow liquor sales on Sunday. It brought to mind the old joke about the Jews not recognizing Christianity, the Christians not recognizing Islam and the Baptists not recognizing each other in the liquor store. That joke offends everyone but like Ricky Gervais says, "I don't care! It's funny!" They sufficed with sodas from the local convenience store. And snickers bars. And Cheetos... It was a moment of celebration and they were going to have a good time regardless of being in a dry county.

Benny got the proposal ready for the broker on the fourplex and emailed it to Ida for her approval. There really wasn't much to it as these things were all fairly standard and it was only about taking care of improvements prior to accepting the transfer of title. In this case, Ida wasn't requiring anything except a slightly lower sale price based on the bids for repairs that Benny had obtained and provided to the selling agent. The money wasn't terribly substantial but it was enough that he expected a counter offer and told Ida to expect that if she approved. Ida felt the offer was actually a bit over what the property was worth but she approved it knowing that to low ball would only anger the seller. In properties such as these the seller generally had a very good idea what their piece was worth and many would take offence at such a thing.

Ida messaged Benny almost immediately and gave the green light for the offer. It was nice that she was so gung-ho on the place, she had asked a lot of questions while looking it over and the disclosure laws in Texas were such that buyers had very good confidence in the taxes, utilities and mold issues often common in these properties. Ida could easily afford such surprises but it's never good to overlook the possibility. Ida had only to go through and e-sign the offer in order for Benny to send it over to the other agent. It wasn't long before his phone notified him the email had arrived and he used Jake's laptop to examine and send it along to the seller.

Technology had made these transactions so much faster and the deal could actually be done today except for the title search. That was such a scam. Pocket change for Ida; an entire industry was built on it and they had to play by the rules. That could take as much as two weeks but Jake and Benny were hoping to be long gone well ahead of that. If they weren't, they could find out about Benny's bogus real estate license. In fact, Benny was thinking he should slow the roll just a bit in order to afford them time to make their date with the cash in Ida's safe. He decided to make the selling agent unavailable for a few days for some reason. He had to come up with something that Ida wouldn't question him on, not like health or an ailing relative; something forgettable. It would come to him.

The current plan was to hit Friday night when they knew Ida would be out on the town but of course she was expecting Charles to go with her at this point. Benny would be alone and on his own to do the deed and it would be up to Jake to give him warning if she decided to go home early. That would give Jake an alibi and Benny would be indisposed for some reason; diarrhea was usually good for a Friday night stay at home excuse. No need for witnesses because who wants to witness diarrhea? At this point the forecast was for dry weather and a full moon. Benny preferred no moon and rain; far fewer people would be out and about and there would be less visibility. Benny could always hope for a change in the weather. His biggest concern for the night of the job at this point would be picking the lock on the back gate. It was actually a passage bolt instead of a padlock on the inside which would give him access to it. But it would also leave him exposed in the alley while he used his tools.

They'd reserved a rental scooter with a luggage box on the back and found a place to park it in the back along Ida's property line. A helmet over the license plate would protect the name on the rental agreement and it was doubtful it would be stolen, especially if Benny took it inside the gate after picking the lock. The plan was a bit more complicated than what they usually had to deal, but it was looking more and more like a sure thing. Benny waited until Thursday afternoon to send the offer to the selling agent to extend their allowable time frame just a smidge. That would take them through the weekend at least.

He also got the same C320 for Jake to woo Miss Ida on Friday night. His friend of a friend tried to charge extra for the favor of the same unit but Benny suggested he might have to go to the dealership body shop and speak to the manager. It would ruin the plan for the same vehicle but there's always a story to cover their butts; like a fender bender. Speaking to the body shop manager was not palatable to the gentleman providing the vehicle and although he was terribly angered at Benny's slight subterfuge, he couldn't pass by the money he'd be making. The vehicle was available on time and as expected.

Friday eventually rolled around and the palpable feeling of excitement made Benny's heart pound. He had all the equipment necessary and the plans had been gone over and tweaked as required; although that was precious little. Mostly it would depend on being unseen while Charles kept Ida busy. Jake had splurged a bit on a new shirt, tie and cuff links at a local men's shop On State Highway 75 that was known for quality for a good price. Charles left to pick up Ida and this strange little man dressed all in black with a black helmet on a black scooter followed him down the road like a dog on a leash behind the black C320. Not the best colors for riding a scooter at night but quite necessary for the job at hand. Had anyone suspected they were together it might have brought a laugh.

Benny parked down the road at the fourplex off to one side of the drive while Jake went up the drive to pick up Ida. It seemed an interminably long time for Charles to be inside with Ida but they eventually reappeared and Charles opened the door for her to enter the vehicle. Benny thought to himself how that could be suggestive of lascivious behavior but maybe that was a bit of jealousy and wishful thinking at the same time. She was indeed a most desirable woman. As the two drove off into the night of debauchery and romance, Benny drove up to the guard shack like clockwork and pulled the scooter around the side where it was hidden by the bushes. He had his equipment in a small pack on his back that he took off once inside the shack. The light was on a timer and had turned on already but that was not an issue for Benny as the bottom of the window was almost at his eye level. One of the few advantages of being small, just like when Le Roy's boys had tried to waist him.

He plugged in the wireless jammer, He checked for the available networks before he turned it on and made a note of the names. He'd need to check those once he got to the house. It was convenient he wouldn't have to write those down with his memory as it was. He was done here for now until he cleaned up his mess after the fact. He had learned a long time ago not to leave behind any clues if he could possibly help it. He stepped around the side of the guard shack and removed his stocking cap to ride around back. Just then a car pulled into the drive and he froze. The headlights obscured the type of vehicle and he couldn't see any lights on the top. To his incredible relief the vehicle was just turning around and it was soon gone down the road. He decided to go pee before pulling the scooter around back. He'd almost done so involuntarily.

Charles and Ida pulled into Arthur's and found a spot not too far from the door. Charles had offered to drop Ida at the door but she had refused claiming that would deny her the walk through the parking lot holding his hand. It was strange and magical the way they bonded and it was such a perfect fit. Jake had never been so inclined toward any woman before and Charles was most certainly enamored. It was a strange mix of desire, protection, aspiration, self-preservation and emotional turmoil all at once. This was completely new to Jake and Charles was all tangled up in the moment. Jake, knowing he had to keep his distance and his head about him while Charles was all about making this woman his own. The conflict in his mind and heart was a terrible nightmarish struggle for control. Even so he kept his wits about him and kept Ida engrossed in conversation while they found a seat in the main dining area and began their meal.

He'd never seen Ida go braless and she was sporting her breasts proudly in the almost shear top she'd chosen; although she was wearing a camisole and nipple covers, she was showing enough that everyone noticed she was trolling for Charle's attention. She had never had children but Charles suspected that she might still have had a little augmentation work done. Jake's mother had taught him that legs are for men and breasts are for babies but, DAMN! He just couldn't help himself to be stimulated by someone already so very attractive. He almost wondered who the mark really was in this game.

Benny rode the scooter out back after emptying his bladder and pulled up just beyond the gate, he removed his helmet and donned the ski mask again. He might look odd to someone driving by but there was also a bush nearby he might try to hide behind; being dressed in all black would help but better to just get this done. It was the worst and most exposed part of the plan. He took his pick tools from his pocket set to work. A good lock pick could do the job in about 30 seconds, Benny started counting and had it done in 40. He could live with that.

The gate opened inward and he moved the scooter inside, closed and locked the gate. He didn't want anything to look out of place so it all had to go back the way it started. The yard was long so he decided to ride the scooter up to the house. He parked it on the side of the electric meter where he cut the security tag and pulled his tools from his bag to loosen the bolt on the securing band. The band fell to the ground and he pulled the meter. There was the distinct tell-tale sound of electricity arcing as something was drawing enough juice to account for several amperes; this hot and sultry time of year it was almost guaranteed to be the air conditioners. He placed the meter on the ground below its mount, turned the scooter around for a quick getaway and walked around to the back porch to check the cameras. There was no tell-tale glow of infrared lights from the camera faces. The system was off and he could remove the ski mask. His timer started now because someone might notice the lights being out here but nowhere else in the neighborhood. That could raise eyebrows and consequently to call the cops to investigate. He wanted to be done in an hour or less, preferably 30 minutes.

He checked his phone for available wireless networks and to his disappointment, they all remained active. Ida likely had hers on a backup battery. He didn't want to have to locate it and disable it after he got inside because the alarm would sound as soon as he opened the door. He opted to look for it outside. Because the internet was still active, he walked around the perimeter of the house to find where it entered the wall. These internet companies had a policy or something that the technicians never penetrated the house up high where it was inaccessible. It was still a stretch for Benny but he found the penetration about six feet up and snipped the wires. He checked his phone again and I.twinkle was now offline. It made sense and he wondered why he hadn't made the connection previously. Ida Periwinkle? Twinkle? Ya, she was the cutsie type and he almost felt bad for what he was about to do. Almost, being the key word.

Charles and Ida had a drink and shared a shrimp cocktail to start he evening while they waited for the entrée. They'd both chosen a filet minion but Charles liked his rare and Ida, medium well.

They came with sautéed asparagus and a baked potato for which they'd both opted to have the works on the potato. How else does one have a baked potato if not with the works? Knowing Ida, Charles expected her to leave a good half of hers behind. Charles ordered for Jim Benny as well telling Ida he felt badly that Jim was under the weather. Ida seemed to melt at Charles seeming heartfelt concern. But she only said that he was a good friend for Jim but she didn't mind having the evening alone with Charles. What could he say? He agreed completely and was enjoying the view with some hope of a magnificent union with Ida before too long. He just wasn't sure tonight would happen once they got back to her place and discovered the imminent result of the con. Their meals arrived in good order and piping hot. The sign of a well-trained staff.

Benny could see the lit alarm panel next to the French doors and knew he had to be quick about disabling it. He'd be very lucky if no other notification had gone out over the internet or cell network already but his experience told him the alarm was the major hurtle. He'd need to open the doors, that would break the magnetic contact starting the countdown to the alarm being activated. These standard alarms had a battery plugged into an outlet and tie strapped to the face plate securing screw. That meant he could just cut the wire between the battery and the control panel as long as the panel had no capacitive back up for power. If it did, it would alert all the right people that would make his night go all wrong. Once the battery was interrupted, he'd just rip the alarm panel from the wall and crush it under his foot. Several times just to be sure. Once the main panel was disabled, the other panels would not be able to communicate. He really hoped that Charles was enjoying his evening while he was here taking all the chances. But Jake's part was important as well and Benny knew he was just feeling jealous about the relationship Charles was having with Ida. Benny counted under his breath, one, two, three! He broke the window in the French door, reached in and unlocked it; he walked in and the alarm started beeping its count down.

Charles was really enjoying the conversation with Ida and couldn't help but let himself get caught up in the moment. Jake would never allow that but he kept telling himself it was necessary to keep Ida on the hook and enjoying herself as well. Ida stopped strangely and took her phone from her tiny hand bag. She shook her head and came back to the conversation. Charles inquired as to the issue and she simply said that power had gone out at the house. Jake was concerned but he didn't want to alarm Ida that this might not be normal. After all, power did go out from time to time especially during the summer heat when usage was high.

Benny had the battery wire to the alarm cut, the panel off the wall and crushed in all of 10 seconds; he pulled the wire used as an antenna as well for good measure. He was par on amazing when the adrenaline was flowing through his blood; like a gazelle, he was poetry in motion. A short fat, bald Gazelle, but a Gazelle none the less. Since the light from the alarm panel no longer lit his way, Benny got out his head light. A light on an elastic strap that many in various trades used to light their way while working in the dark, especially those that explored caves. He pulled the strap around his head and switched it on. That left his hands free for working.

He went up the stairs to Ida's bedroom, there was the door that held so much mystery. It had a pass bolt lock and Benny had to use his lock picking skills again. It was a little faster this time and the door opened to show what they'd hoped to see. The DVR and the safe, both in the same room. It already felt like victory to Benny but he knew he had to stay focused. He only had another fifteen minutes of preferred time to get this done. He grabbed the DVR so there was no mistake or record for the police. He then went about drilling out the tumblers on the cheap unit at which he was looking. Most people, even rich people didn't have the incredibly complex safe units shown in the movies. Most were just run of the mill, just above department store quality.

He was in, in just under two minutes... to nothing. There was nothing in the safe! What the hell! Where was the money? Then he saw the piece of paper folded and sitting on the top shelf. Benny had a very sick feeling in the pit of his stomach as he realized they'd been had. He picked up the note and unfolded it. "Hi boys! I so adore you both! I hope we can be long term friends and that you can help me with a little job that I have planned. No police yet, unless you refuse. I have back up cameras... I'll tell you all about it in the morning! Please put things back the way you found them. Oh, you owe me a safe."
Wasn't that just a kick in the nuts? Benny about puked. He texted Jake, "We've been had; she knows. Have fun on your date but don't say a word."

Charles stopped to look at the incoming message on his phone. When his face went white as a ghost, Ida laughed, loud and long. "Don't worry sweety, we're still going to have a good time tonight! And tomorrow, you'll love me even more."
What does a guy say to that?
"All right, I guess we missed something?"
"Several somethings but that's oaky. My feelings are real and you are the best I've ever met. Are you willing to give it a go?"
"Do I have a choice?"
"No, so you might as well be my boyfriend and we can get this show on the road!"
What could he say? He'd been had, after more than two decades of success, someone had gotten the better of him. They enjoyed the rest of their dinner as much as he could and Ida kept smiling and snickering. She was quite pleased and couldn't help herself.

Benny did as instructed and put everything back as he'd found it. What he could, of course. He closed the door, went back out and replaced the electric meter the best he could. Ran the scooter out to the gate, went out and locked it on the outside. He collected the WIFI jammer so there was no evidence that could be traced back to them. He'd stuffed the note in his pocket to show Jake as he couldn't even believe it himself. Who was this woman that she saw right through them? He rode back to the motel not knowing what to think but this was the first time in his life he was left not knowing his own probable future.

CHAPTER FIVE: THE SWEET SEDUCTION OF THINGS TO COME.

Aside from the snickering every few moments, Ida went easy on Charles. He couldn't even imagine where they'd gone wrong but Ida seemed okay with it. She was still warm, wonderful and full of joy and life which left Charles wondering How he would explain Jake and Benny. At one point during dinner, she even shook her assets at him and told him, you'd better make it a good evening; she then laughed and had to stifle herself she was so self-entertained. Jake was outside of his realm here and although he didn't think she was kidding he still couldn't believe what she was implying. But she was obviously quite pleased with herself and she made no attempt at hiding it.

When dinner was done Ida took him by the hand and told him dinner was on her this evening. She was just beside herself with what had happened and so full of laughter! As they walked outside everyone in the restaurant that knew Ida, was staring at the couple that was so obviously in love. Jake was wondering if she was psychotic? A regular Bonny and Clyde? He guessed he would be finding out.

When they got back to Ida's place, she seemed to be preoccupied with looking around at everything in view. As she opened the front door, she noticed the alarm didn't start beeping right away. "Aha! How good are you at dealing with the police?"

"Well, not really my forte but I can hold my own."

"Okay, just follow my lead."

She immediately dialed 911 and played the part of the shocked and scared woman perfectly. In fact, Jake thought she might actually be a bit shocked but he knew better.

"You might want to use your real name if the police ask. By the way, what is it?"

"Jake."

"I like Charles better but Jake will do. How about you are Jake, but use your middle name of Charles?"

"You're the boss."

"I like that."

When the cops arrived, the neighbors came over to report the lights had been out. Of course, the cops wanted to know why no one had called. Well, it didn't seem important at the time. Both officers turned away from the neighbors and rolled their eyes at Jake and Ida. Ida played it well by covering her smile and both of the officers got a kick from that.

They went into the house and found the French door window broken out and the alarm panel violated so one of them went outside and then called the other officer out to witness the electric meter. They took photos of the scooter tire prints in the moist dirt of the well-watered grass. Something Jake and Benny had not considered but, truly, what were the chances it was the only scooter with that tire? The officers made note of the tire prints from and to the back gate as the point of entry to the yard. Benny's foot prints were plainly visible but non distinct. The only thing the officers could tell was that they were size Seven.

The officers went upstairs and Ida showed them her safe room and unlocked the door to which the officers seemed truly shocked, the perpetrator had actually closed and locked the door behind him/herself. That was odd all by itself. Had not Ida been on a date with Jake Charles, and everyone at Arthur's that knew her and had seen her with Charles, she would be suspect number one and Jake, suspect number two. Jake was beginning to understand the brilliance of her scam. But Benny might have to blow town. The officers took photos of the drill hole in the safe and took a report of the contents... It was a good thing Benny had taken the note that Ida had left. Two million in cash. Jake was curious what insurance company would pay out for cash. Ida would later confide; the insurance company had placed the cash and approved the security. They would have no choice. Oh, so brilliant, this woman! The officers also noted the DVR was missing and asked if there was a backup system to which Ida replied no. Jake knew differently.

The police fingerprint crew had arrived and started dusting for prints of which they found nothing. Jake knew Benny would not be that careless. By two o'clock in the morning, the investigation was over and the officers only recommended that Ida call her insurance in the morning. They gave her a report number to give to her insurance carrier and they were gone faster than they had arrived. Everyone needed a good night's sleep. Jake requested Ida's permission to text Benny of which she was only too happy to approve and he let Benny know he'd call him in the morning. Benny texted back a smiley face and a thumbs up. The night was about to get even more interesting.

The morning arrived at Ten a.m. but the curtains in In Ida's bedroom were room darkening with valences to keep the sunlight from creeping over the top. Ida was already up and Charles could smell the coffee brewing. He had not expected that from Ida but it was quite welcome. She'd laid out a towel for him with which to dry off after he showered so he took advantage of the expectation but was quick about it. He was in and out in under ten minutes and dressed in under five. He made the bed they had so expertly torn to pieces and found his way down to the kitchen where Ida was buttering some toast to put beside the eggs and bacon she'd prepared. Charles had seldom been treated so well since his mother had passed and he simply could not imagine what was going through this woman's mind. He decided to play on the moment and walked up to hug her. To his pleasure she turned and kissed him first and then wrapped her arms around him. This was the stuff from which fantasy novels were written. But he had to know, "Ida, how did you know about Jim and me?"

"Let's leave that for later so Jim can be here and I only have to explain it once. For right now, let's just say you did almost everything right; except to start to fall in love with me."

"You realized that too?"

"It was very obvious and quite honestly, welcome. I've never met anyone quite like you. Such a gentleman that loved his mother so much. I just had to pull you in and see if those feelings might come my way. And they did. You were telling me the truth about your mom, right?"

"Yes, she always treated me very well, through all of her many terrible flaws she was always there for me. I never doubted for a moment that she loved me."

"And you will never have to doubt for a moment that I love you as well. That's one reason you and Jim are not sitting in jail for breaking and entering. I was actually amazed at how little damage was done to get in here. Hey, I've already called the insurance people, do you care to stick around and hear what they have to say? It might be interesting for you…"

"You know, that doesn't sound half bad. I've never witnessed what happens after one of my little jobs."

"Honey, that was no little job, even though my system wasn't top of the line, you boys got past some very sophisticated systems. The insurance carrier even approved them. Although next time, the cameras will be on a battery backup. But your plan even foiled that aspect. Especially taking the DVR. Maybe I'll put that in a different location in case there's a next time."

"Probably not a bad idea. We couldn't tell where it might be, other than with the safe. Of course, all your wires lead right to it, and you don't want to have to reroute all of those. Maybe a plate steel cover to keep it safer?"

"I'll take it under consideration. After you boys return it to me?"
"After we erase the hard drive…"
"What? You don't trust me?" Ida laughed a lilting tease to which Charles could only smile.
"I think after all of this I probably do, but I'm still not one to take chances."
"It's a good thing my backup cameras are connected elsewhere."
"Ya, about those…"
"Nope, no way, not yet."
"Okay."

At that moment the doorbell rang and Ida excused herself to go and see who it was. Charles could hear conversation from the doorway and gathered it was the insurance investigator. They were johnny on the spot for a two-million-dollar claim, plus damages…
"Mr. Johnson, this is my boyfriend, Charles Gordon."
"It's a pleasure to meet you Mr. Johnson."
"The pleasure's all mine Mr. Gordon. I take it that's your Mercedes in the drive?"
"Yes, I've had it only a short time. Nice vehicle to get around town."
"I'm sure it is."
"Mrs. Periwinkle, I've already obtained and read the police report, mostly, I just need photographs of our own for the underwriters. Could you show me around? Let's start with the point of entry."
They both accompanied Mr. Johnson to the back door where Ida showed him the broken glass, the back gate, the scooter tracks and the electric meter.
"Have you called the electric company to replace their security band on the meter?"
"I hadn't thought of that."
"They'll want to get that done right away. You probably ought to call them right after I'm done here."
"Of course."

"Did your alarm send you a message about the power going out?"

"Yes."

"You didn't find that strange?"

"Not this time year when there is so much draw on the grid."

"Makes sense."

Mr. Johnson was very professional and although some of his questions seemed accusatory, he didn't pursue any line of questions that might indicate he was suspicious. He took a lot of photos, more thought Charles, than were warranted, but he didn't know the man's business and for what he might need them.

"I understand you two were out to dinner at the time?"

"Yes, we go to Arther's fairly regularly."

"If I go there and ask, will there be anyone that remembers you?"

"Mr. Johnson, I understand you have to examine all possibilities but you can't expect us to be able to tell you what someone else will remember."

"No, I suppose that's true, but possibly you spoke to someone that you see often? I'm sorry to be this way, I just have to confirm every aspect of what might have happened."

"Of course. Maybe the bartender," responded Charles. "I don't know him by name but he generally recognizes and acknowledges everyone in the place."

"I can imagine, I'll ask him if he remembers you."

"Just a moment Mr. Johnson, I paid on my debit card, let me see if the receipt is in my purse."

"That would save me a trip out there if you still have it."

Ida got her bag and checked. It was indeed there.

"Let me make a copy of this for you, I need the original in case of any other questions."

"Of course."

Ida walked over to her office and Charles could hear her all-in-one fire up, scan and then print the copy.

"Here you are Mr. Johnson," the photo copy fluttering as Ida breezed back into the room.

"Thank you, Mrs. Periwinkle. I'm glad it's a fresh thermal receipt,

they often fade with time. Let's go assess the safe and such."
Ida led the way up to her room; Charles was embarrassed he
hadn't made the bed before the inspector had arrived.
"Do you normally keep this door locked?"
"Always."
"And you are the only one with a key?"
"Yes."
"Do you have a spare?"
"In the office down stairs."
"I'll need you to show that to me along with your regular key on
the way out."
"Certainly."
"This is interesting, your burglar broke the window in the door,
cut the wire and destroyed the alarm panel to get in but picked
this lock. He even put the electric meter back in place before
riding off. Instead of just cutting the wires on the back of the
DVR he unplugged everything, meticulously. He seems to have
been in a hurry to get in but took his time to do everything
in a pristine manner up here. I'll have to run this by my police
psychologist friend."
"Would you let me know what the psychologist says? Sounds
interesting to me also," said Ida.
"I'll make a note of it and give you a call."
"Thank you."
Mr. Johnson wrote a note on his report to do just that.
After taking a couple of dozen more photos, Johnson seemed
satisfied he'd caught every angle. He mentioned the police report
noted they had dusted for prints with no joy. He said they don't
usually find any but there's always the off chance they might
get lucky. Charles thought to himself that he'd gotten lucky last
night and the Mona Lisa grin on Ida's face told him that great
minds run in the same gutters.

They headed down to the office where Ida pulled her normal set
of keys from her hand bag and showed Johnson the extra key
she kept high on a book shelf, the two keys matched and had

the name of the lock manufacturer stamped into them. He had Ida place the keys on her desk and he photographed those as well. Johnson seemed satisfied with his inspection at this point and excused himself to go back to the office to write his report. On his way out he mentioned the underwriters might call with questions of their own.

"Well, he was quite thorough," was Charle's only remark.
"He just about upset me with some of his questions. I had to remind myself that he had to consider all possibilities; especially where cash was concerned." The company was going to balk at paying on a loss of cash anyway as without the DVR there was no way to know if Ida herself had taken the money. She would likely have to sue for a settlement of some type and that always took time. But the boys had been very efficient in taking the DVR and that broke the most valuable link in the chain of evidence. Aside from her note, there was nothing that could have gone wrong. Ida kicked herself a bit for the note but that was like icing on the cake for her to goad her new friends with. It also made her feel like she was in control to an extent. She wasn't normally that person, but it felt good this time. Almost like she had put herself in the position of the ring leader.

Charles had to call Benny, he asked if Ida would mind him filling in his friend on everything. She had no issue, after all they were now partners in crime and they had to keep each other up to date. She was wondering how Jim would take the news and it wasn't long before Charles gave her his report. She had to laugh several times at Jim's wonderment about the whole affair but the part that really made her laugh was his request to move in with her.
"You are kidding me!" she exclaimed.
"No, no. He thinks that if we are going to be a gang of thieves and because we got nothing for our investment you should probably allow us to move in with you and save us the money on the hotel."

"Seriously? Is that how you feel about it?"

"I more hope you will, because we have a relationship."

"Well, give me a moment to think about it. Moment's up. You can move in today, but I get final say in all decisions concerning 'our' home and I lead our first caper. Is that even your Mercedes parked in my driveway?"

"I bought a very nondescript Caprice from the Nissan Dealer on I-635 on the way into town. The C320 is a rental or maybe a loaner owned by the dealership up State Highway 75. Jim knows someone that knows someone."

"I wondered if you would tell me the truth. I pulled records from the DMV when we first met, I know someone that knows someone. I knew you didn't own it. One of your mistakes although that was an acceptable faux pas. The fact that you came clean on that is to your credit. It would have been a huge mistake to lie to me at this point," Ida said with a grin like the cat that caught the canary. Charles knew he'd met his match and had no intention of misleading Ida any more. Especially as she was showing him how much she'd been ahead of their game all along.

"You can park your caprice off to the side of the drive and buy a car cover."

"I won't be keeping it long, I bought it with fake I.D. and will need to abandon it somewhere."

"Somewhere other than this neighborhood, please," Ida said that looking at him sideways.

"Of course."

During their conversation, Charles had texted Benny a simple 'yes, move' to indicate that Ida was okay with them moving in. Benny had already packed his things and only had to pack things for Jake and collect the unused part of their rent from the hotel. He was already champing at the bit to hit the road when Jake's cryptic message came through and he jumped into the Caprice and turned the key. The car fired right up and Benny threw it into reverse to back out of the parking space. As he came about and stopped to shift into drive, he noticed a car he recognized sitting backed in at the end of the lot. It was the same car that did the drive by to try and kill him. His heart raced and climbed into his throat. The first thing he did was to tell himself not to panic… Easier said than done. He knew these guys meant business and the last thing he wanted to do was lead them to Ida's place. The first thing that crossed his mind was trying to run but that might prove fatal when avoiding a gang with guns in traffic. His second thought was to go back into the hotel lobby to call the cops but he quickly dismissed that idea as being fatally flawed as well. Nothing worse than being a stationary target. He started driving forward at a moderate pace so as not to alert them that he'd seen them; there were four in the car. Enough to shoot from each window. He decided the best course of action was to get to the closest cop shop as quickly as possible and get the plate number from the other vehicle if they got close enough. Benny called 911 and gave the operator his location and concern. Of course, she wanted him to stay put and he told her she was smoking really good crack. That was not appreciated. He promised to stay on the phone with her so a patrol car could find him. The operator said they couldn't find him if he was moving and she didn't like his next response either.

"Lady, we both know you cops can track my phone to within a half a block if you want to. I'm moving onto the surface roads now and I'll be on the highway in less than a mile. I know your guys can find me in a beige Caprice followed by Blue Chevy Chevelle before I hit the highway."

"Sir, Please, stay where you are!"

"Ma'am, tell your guys to get it into gear right now!"

Before Benny got a block down the street, a patrol car pulled in behind him and lit him up with a second one waiting for the Chevelle. The gang bangers stopped in the middle of the road and all four fled in different directions with the car running. There was no catching them at that point as it was a one-way access road beside the highway and the patrol car had to go around the block to get in behind the Chevelle. The officer in the second car simply drove around the block to direct traffic around the parked vehicle while waiting on a tow truck. Benny, however, was detained for questioning under such suspicious circumstances at the local hamburger joint parking lot. He wasn't very happy about that and let the first cop know about it in no uncertain terms but then thanked him for being there and probably saving his life. So, Jim Benny gave the officer his information and a full report of how this had all gone down, about Lee Roy, the drive by shooting, his time camping out at the pipe and the time hiding out at the hotel. Of course, the cop wanted to know whose car he was driving and Benny could only say it belonged to his friend Jake. The officer ran the plates and although he was not impressed by it not being reregistered yet after purchase, the 30 days weren't up and it didn't come back as stolen; so, there wasn't much he could do about it. It took an hour for Benny to convince the officer there was nothing going on that warranted any further investigation but he finally accepted His story and let him go about his business. Besides, who wouldn't believe little four-foot eleven-inch Jim Benny? Especially after the behavior of the guys in the Chevelle.

Benny finally got to Ida's place and parked the car right where Ida instructed him to do so. She was out the door in a heartbeat to point to the spot as she just couldn't have the neighbors seeing that old hunk a junk sitting there. Benny called her a snob and she just said, "Yes." They both laughed.
"Hey, Ida, thanks for letting us stay here. Have I got a story for you and Jake!"
"Oh, he's going to go by Charles from now on because I like the name better."
"Pussy whipped, is what he is."
"Yes," she said again and they both laughed again.
Ida helped Charles and Jim carry their things into the house so she proved that she couldn't be too much of a snob. She gave Benny the guest room on the main floor and told Charles she would be giving him a drawer in her room to which Benny put his hand to his mouth and faux coughed, "Pussy whipped." To

which they all laughed and Charles said, "Guilty!"

Benny proceeded to relate the story of his pursuers and the subsequent interrogation by the cop in the parking lot. Ida was concerned there may have been a second car of thugs that followed him to her place. Benny reassured her that he had gone the scenic route to throw off any one hanging back to follow him. "By the way, Jim," said Ida, what is your real name?"

"Ya, I've never known your real first name, Benny."

"It's Jim," replied Benny. "Jim Benny."

"Seriously?" inquired Charles.

"Seriously," replied Benny.

"Aren't you full of surprises?" Ida feigned shock.

"Not really and I prefer to keep it that way. That's why I try and keep everything simple"

"Then why did you snitch on Lee Roy?" asked Ida.

"But I didn't! I've got no clue where that came from!"

"By the time we're done with him, he'll be wishing he'd never heard your name," said Ida.

"What are you talking about?" inquired Benny.

"He's going to be our first mark."

Charles and Benny booth stood stunned and mouths agape. Ida just laughed at them both as they stood there wondering if she might be psychotic.

"Are you nuts?" decried Jim.

"What the hell?" followed Charles.

More laughter from Ida, and then again, "Yes! Who better to con than a criminal? He can't go to the police and if everything works out right, he'll go away for 25 to life."

Charles and Jim together, "If?"

"Well, nothing is guaranteed."

CHAPTER SIX: THE BACK STORY

No one ever knew how old man Periwinkle had come by his money. His was an old family in Dallas and many said that it was from running shine, others figured it was oil and even more thought he had his fingers into the Louisiana cassinos. Truth was, it was a bit of all three and even much more. He appeared to most to be a kindly older gent with nary a bad bone in his body but the truth was, he was as mean and vicious as any gangster if anyone dared step into his business. Especially today's wanna-be gangsters that sagged their pants, held their pistols sideways and couldn't hit the side of a barn with both eyes on the target. He had a special hatred of the low life hood rats that were taking over the South, even infiltrating his grandfather's loan sharking enterprises. His grandfather had started him at the age of ten running money for the mob in Shreveport. He was tall for his age and extremely fast on his feet, especially when being chased by the competition.

Although his grandfather loved little Max Periwinkle III, he knew grandpa saw him as expendable More by necessity than by any streak of mean. It was just business; as much as grandpa loved him, business was business and he had to be the best if he was to take grandpa's place. His father, Max Jr., had been good but not good enough to outrun a bullet when Max was only six years old. Max had a great deal to learn and being faster than a bullet would be part of his training. The gangster world in which he was growing up was lethal but lucrative and there was no denying it had been good to the senior Periwinkle; Max intended to be even more successful.

Moonshine had become less than necessary after prohibition but it was still popular and Max III kept that business going simply as another means of income regardless of it being low key these days. Everyone these days was into the Apple Jack and Peach Cobler flavored crap and he supposed if they wanted it, he'd make it happen. He used that money to invest in oil futures and other aspects of oil that were legal and could launder those gains. From time to time, he bought into his friend's casinos and helped them grow but they were becoming less inclined to let him leach off of their success as they no longer needed the front money like they had back in the day. Loan sharking was becoming less of a business because of the expense of collection from the less and less trustworthy criminal element that needed that type of money. That business was falling more to the drug syndicates that already had people on the streets collecting for the drugs.

Then one night while walking back to his Shreveport apartment from a back-room game of poker, a young punk black kid dressed in rags with a red bandana wrapped around his head thought he would be stupid and pull a gun on Max. The teenager wasn't more than fifteen and Max knew he couldn't hit crap holding it sideways the way he did. He wrested the weapon form him in less than a half second and pointed it right in his face. Then stepped back so the kid couldn't take it back. Max made him get down on his knees and the kid started pissing his pants. Max just shook his head, it wasn't worth catching a case for killing this coward so he asked, "What's your name kid?"
Begrudgingly he answered, "Lee Roy Pope."
"Have you got any connections around here?"
"What kind of connections you talking about?"
"Any kind! Just answer the God Damned question!"
"Ya, a few."

"A few, huh?" Max took the magazine from the weapon and ejected the cartridge from the chamber. "I've got a front office over on Third Avenue, 'Max Loans'. Come by there tomorrow around ten if you really have connections. I need someone just as brave as they are stupid. Ask for Max."

He gave the weapon back to Lee Roy and put the magazine into his pocket. "You can have this back tomorrow if you show up. Oh, dress for success if you got the threads."

"No one uses that word anymore."

"Well, I do."

He then just walked on like it was a typical evening. Lee Roy stood there looking after him, dumbfounded and confused about what had just happened. Then he went home to change his pants.

Lee Roy showed up at Max's office at ten on the nose and walked in. "May I help you?" asked the incredibly gorgeous brunette behind the desk in the waiting area.

"Ya, I was told to ask for Max."

"Oh, so you're the young man he told me about. Well, Max, I'm Mr. Periwinkle's secretary. You may call me Ida. I'll be your main contact as Mr. Periwinkle isn't always available. So, remember my name."

"Yes, Miss Ida."

"Mmm, manners as well as guts. Let's keep it that way, shall we?"

"Yes, Miss Ida."

Ida rose and turned in the tight office space and knocked on Max's door.

"Yes?"

"Your young man is here to see you."

"Damn, on time as well. Send him in, Ida"

Ida opened the door a bit more and said, "You may go in to see Mr. Periwinkle now."

"Pretty ballsy of you to get in here. I like that. Here's your magazine as promised. Ida has the cartridges and you can have those on your way out the door."

"Yes, sir, Mr. Periwinkle."

"You catch on fast about respect, don't you?"

"You let me live, that's worth something."

"Yes, it certainly is. Close the door."

"You don't trust your girl?"

Max paused and looked Lee Roy up and down for a moment. This young man had a mouth, but it was a reasonable question.

"If I didn't rust her, she wouldn't work for me. I just don't involve her if I don't have to. Plausible deniability for her. Do you understand what that means?"

"Yes, sir. She don't know what she don't need to know and she can't roll on you."

"Good. It protects her as well, if she doesn't know, she isn't as likely to catch a case."

"Makes sense. You ain't like no gangster I ever knew before. It's like you got a code or something."

"Or something. I'm as mean as any junk yard dog ever was if you cross me. Don't think for a moment that I'm not. But my grandpa taught me to respect even my enemies and they're less likely to turn on a person."

"Okay, I can dig it."

"Can you? You want a job? It's not legal and it's not safe but it pays a thousand a week to start."

"Oh, hell yes!"

"You need some cash up front for food and such?"

"My momma, she drinks a bit. Don't hold it against her, she can't help herself since Daddy left last year. But I could use it for food for her, me and my little sister if you don't mind."

"I'll front you a thousand then, but it comes out of your weekly pay $200 a week until it's paid off. You understand? If you don't show up tomorrow, don't ever let me see you again 'cause I'll find a way to burn you."

"Yes, sir. Thank you, sir."

"We don't keep track of what we pay you; you're an independent contractor. You pay or don't pay taxes as you see fit. That's between you and the real criminals, the government. Don't ever include me in your taxes if you choose to file. You are a contractor; I've got no record of the expenditure."

"Of course, Mr. Periwinkle"

Max stood and Lee Roy stood at the same time, the show of respect was not lost on Max.

"Go ahead and let yourself out the door but wait in the outer office."

"Yes, sir."

Lee Roy left the office and Max called in Ida. He explained the pay agreement and the front money repayment. He reminded her to give him his ammo on his way out the front door.

"All right, Lee Roy. I'll get your money and your other items, give me just a moment."

"Yes, Miss Ida."

Ida unlocked what sounded to be a safe in the floor under her desk. It was a good thing she was lean and could bend down like that, she popped back up with ten Benjamins in her hand and the ammo as well.

"You'll be paid every Friday at noon before we close for the day, we go home early on Fridays. Don't be late and don't forget it or you'll wait until Monday to be paid"

"Thank you, Miss Ida."

"You're welcome, Lee Roy. I can assume we'll see you tomorrow at 9am sharp?"

"Oh, yes, Miss Ida. For sure!"

"Okay then, have a nice morning and don't spend that all in one place."

"Yes, Miss Ida... I mean no, Miss Ida... Damn, you know what I mean."

"Language Mr. Pope."

She smiled and Lee Roy laughed. "Good day Miss Ida."

"Call Georgy for me will you, Ida?"

"Yes, Mr. Periwinkle."

Ida had only heard rumors around the area but she believed Georgy was heavy into the cocaine trade around town. She wondered what Max had in mind. She wondered, but didn't really want to know.

The next morning, Lee Roy showed up on time and dressed a bit better. He wasn't overdressed but he had spent a little of the money Max had fronted him on a new shirt and kicks. Not the Hundred-fifty-dollar kicks either. Just some nice clean Thirty-dollar models that looked a bit better.

"Very nice, Lee Roy," said Ida as she looked him up and down.

"Yes, Miss Ida. I had a little left over after buying groceries for the week. I still got some left in case we have an emergency."

"Good planning on your part, Lee Roy. Mr. Periwinkle isn't here this morning, he had business across town but he left instructions. You are to take this bag to the address on this paper. Do not look inside the bag, do not stop anywhere and do not talk to anyone. It will take twelve minutes to go from here to that address, five minutes to drop it and come back with a bag they will give you; you will not look inside that bag either. You will come back at three this afternoon and do the same thing again."

"A split shift? That ain't right."

"That's all you will do every day this this week for your money except for Friday when we go home early, is that going to be a problem?"

"No, Miss Ida. Sorry for complaining."

"I understand; things will change along the way and you will be given more responsibility if you complete your tasks as instructed. Now get along your way before I have to give a demerit."

"Demerits, Miss Ida?"

She smiled and winked at him and went about her filing which he had interrupted.

"Yes, Miss Ida."

Lee Roy was out the door and whistling as he went. Ida didn't hear much of the tune but it didn't sound like anything she'd ever heard before. Lee Roy was humming the same tune when he came back through the door almost exactly a half hour later.

He handed Ida the bag and turned to walk out the door when Ida mentioned, "Three o'clock then?"

"Yes, Miss Ida."

"Very good."

Lee Roy didn't terry but he did note in the corner of his eye that Miss Ida appeared to put the bag into the assumed floor safe.

This continued through the week and on Thursday Ida suggested he might consider changing his route slightly so the neighborhood wouldn't get used to seeing him walking the same one every day twice a day.

"Already ahead of you on that, Miss Ida. But thanks anyway. One of my home boys mentioned seeing me a lot of me the other day so I fixed that already. I can guess pretty much what I'm doing for Mr. Periwinkle and Georgy and the last thing I need is to get rolled for either bag."

"You are wise for your years, young man. I've already spoken to Mr. Periwinkle and your schedule will change up next week but it will be the same job. We'll let you know come Monday how we want it done. For the next week."

"All right, Miss Ida. I'll see you in the morning. Can I get paid at that time or do you want me to come back at noon?"

"I spoke with Mr. Periwinkle and he said to pay you when you return with the second bag in the morning."

"You right on top of things, Miss Ida!"

"And that's why all that know me, love me."

"You alright in my book. Thanks again."

"You're welcome, Lee Roy."

Lee Roy had to wonder how Miss Ida had gotten tangled up with Max Periwinkle III because the word around town was that he was the worst of the worst if one crossed him. He'd been warned upon having mentioning the Periwinkle name that he should steer clear of him. Miss Ida seemed so sweet and smart it just didn't make much sense. Not that it was really any of his business, it was just something he had to wonder about and he kind of wanted to ask. But that opportunity didn't seem to present itself as Miss Ida kept him at arm's length and all business when he entered the office. She was certainly very nice about it but it was very clear that there was no fraternizing, not even just the friendly chit chat kind. He really wanted to know more but figured he'd need to just wait and see if they brought him into their circle of trust.

Lee Roy made his last drop for the week on Friday morning and this time Mr. Periwinkle was in the office and invited Lee Roy in to see him.
"Yes, Mr. Periwinkle. What can I do for you, sir."
"Ida has already told you we're going to change things up a bit next week, Are you okay with the job so far?"
"Yes, sir."
"You already have it figured out, haven't you?"
"It ain't hard to guess."
"No, I suppose not. How's your family doing, you all getting enough to eat?"
"Yes, sir. And momma's trying to cut back on her drinking. All on her own without no help and me not asking her too. It seems she just was worrying too much about how to make ends meet and then spending it on booze to numb her pain. She ain't dry yet but things are a whole lot better since you gave me a job."
"That's what I like to hear. Okay, you know we close early today, don't be hanging out around here this weekend, go and have some fun, and be with your family as well. Family always comes first, even in our world around here. You go home and see if you can stay out of trouble this weekend."
"Yes, sir, Mr. Periwinkle."
"Okay, go get your week's pay from Ida."
"Thanks, Mr. Periwinkle. You have a good weekend too."
Max just nodded affirmation and watched as Lee Roy got his money and said goodbye to Ida for the weekend. He was not yet impressed with the young man but he was feeling it was the right thing to do and that it might work out well for them all. At noon, he and Ida set the alarm and locked up. They walked down

the street together until they reached Max's car.

"What do you think of our young man, Ida?"

"I can't really say Mr. Periwinkle but he seems to be happy and willing to do whatever you ask of him."

"Yes, he does. Well, time will tell. Here comes your bus. When are you going to buy a car? Lord knows I pay you enough."

"When you let me start calling you Max!" she said with a smile.

Max smiled at that as he'd done so long ago.

"All right, go enjoy your weekend. Think about it?"

"I do quite often. You're really doing a good thing for Lee Roy. You may have convinced me with this."

Max had asked Ida to marry him some time ago and she had said then, when you start letting me call you Max. She was mostly concerned with what his kids would think and he had spoken with them. They were not completely convinced it was the right thing to do but their mother had passed almost fifteen years ago and they just wanted their father to be happy. They sat on it for a while but finally gave their blessing on the union. Ida still didn't want to jump right into it; he was twenty years her senior and it was a crime family. Still, they treated her well and with respect. Maybe come Monday she'd start calling him Max.

The weekend rolled past far too quickly as do most weekends and Max was in the office early as was Ida come Monday morning. A box was delivered by currier and Max took it into his office and closed the door, shut the shades. Ida had her suspicions but kept her opinion to herself. When Lee Roy arrived, Max came out of his office and gave him his written instructions along with a small box with three packages in it.

"Do you have a license yet? Of course not, you're only fifteen."

"I got my learner's permit, Mr. Periwinkle."

"Okay, that should do. I'll check with my attorney; you're going to need to have transportation. It won't be fancy, not even a car but I think the law says you can ride a scooter at fifteen."

"Yes, sir. It does."

"All right, I've got something lined up. You can't be walking the streets with your new responsibilities."

"Stick around when you come back."

"Yes, sir."

"I've got to go out for a bit, Ida. Keep Lee Roy entertained until I get back."

"My pleasure, Max."

Lee Roy and Max both stopped dead in their tracks as that had never before been heard in that office. Max smiled and Ida smiled back. Lee Roy knew he was missing something but went about his business without asking. Max took his hat and coat and left he office with a bit of a hop in his giddy up.

When Max returned Lee Roy was sitting in the outer office and Ida was having an animated conversation with him about this family and their weekend. He'd treated them all to a hamburger at the local fast-food joint and a matinee. Something they used to do when his daddy was alive. He was telling how happy his momma was and how she finally seemed to be finding her old laughter again. She was still drinking but Lee Roy reported it was only a few nights a week and not nearly as much as it used to be. Max walked in just in time to hear that part and he encouraged Lee Roy to just give her time and encouragement. Not to be upset if she back slid.

"Yes, sir, Mr. Periwinkle."

"Your scooter should be here shortly. Well, my scooter technically but the one you'll be using. Show me you can do the job and I'll look at giving you a small raise next month, very small. You're making enough money for me that I can afford it."

"Yes, Sir! Mr. Periwinkle!"

With that Max retired to his office and shut the door.

When the scooter arrived, it was a new 175cc model with a trunk, all in black with a black helmet as well.

"They don't let these on the highways so you're limited to the surface roads," the delivery man told him. "And you will get it towed if you don't wear your helmet at your age."

Lee Roy was beside himself and couldn't believe Mr. Periwinkle had done this for him.

"Thanks, I'll be sure to wear it all the time. I like my head just the way it is."

"It's got a full tank and it purrs like a kitten. Don't ride it too hard at first 'cause the piston rings need to seat in to the cylinder. All right, the rest is up to you. Be careful."

"Thank you, Mr.!"

"I guess I should have asked if you have a place to store that before I bought it," Max had come out to great his friend that delivered the scooter.

"My friend has a shed in his back yard, he'll let me keep it in there."

"Okay, but you're the only one that rides it."

"No problem, Mr. Periwinkle. He has one of his own."

"Okay, go out and practice riding a bit but be back at two today, you have five deliveries."

"Yes, sir! Mr. Periwinkle sir!"

Lee Roy dawned his helmet and headed out like he'd ridden hist entire life. Max just said, "Humph," And went back into his office. Ida followed him in this time and sat down across from Max with her legs and arms crossed. She was smiling like the cheshire cat and Max couldn't help but smile back.

"I think your just an old softy."

"Maybe, but that's just between you and me. This is strictly business if anyone asks."

"Of course it is."

"Speaking of business, would you join me at Ruth's Chris Steak House tonight for dinner?"

"I'd love too. Is what I'm wearing okay?"

"You'd look lovely in a burlap sack. But I don't suggest it, I hear they itch."

"Have you told your kids yet?"

"First thing I did. They seemed happy enough. You know how they are."

"It's understandable, but they have nothing to worry about. You know I'll sign a prenup if that's what they want."

"They do. Are you sure that's okay?"

"Yes, we've known each other for almost ten years. It's just business." She smiled at that and so did Max. It was their little joke it had been said so many times.

"My attorney is drawing it up and should have it by next week. Do you realize you need to have your own attorney look at it?"

"Yes, it's one of those formalities that is required to make it legal."

"Okay, well, get back to work. I'm not paying you to sit around and jabber all day long"

Max sat back in his chair and Ida went back to her busy work humming the wedding march.

"Oh, stop it, must you be so damned cheerful all the time."

"Yes, Max, I must."

Max got up and quietly closed the door so he could make some phone calls.

When Lee Roy returned, he was right on time again and again Max had his deliveries boxed up and ready to go. He even took them out and placed them in the trunk on the scooter as he chatted with Lee Roy. "Here's the addresses and you might want to get a phone holder to put on your handle bars so you can use it for a GPS. You'll be going places you might not have been to before."

"Yes, Mr. Periwinkle."

"And be aware of your surroundings, it won't be long before unsavory types start noticing you. Have you ever had any fight training?"

"Just what I've learned from the streets."

"Starting this weekend, I want to go see Franky over at Franky's Do Jo. I've already made arrangements for him to personally train you in mixed martial arts and boxing."

"I'd rather just have a gun, Mr. Periwinkle."

"I know but that's a great way to get dead. Do you know the three rules of a gun fight?"

"No, what rules?"

"Exactly, you don't know jack. They are: run, hide and then fight at the last resort."

"But that ain't what you did with me."

"You were a punk kid and I taught you a lesson. By the time Franky gets done with you, you won't be a punk anymore."

"I can't believe you just said that to me!"

"Believe it. You've got a lot to learn about being the man you need to be in this business. Especially if you want to be respected and honorable as well."

"All right, I'll give you a pass this time."

Max just smiled; he was beginning to like Lee Roy. He had spunk, character, respect and he was proving himself an asset. Ida had also taken a shine to him. They were becoming a family of sorts.

Max had tried to bring his own son and daughter into the family business but regardless of what he said or did, they simply didn't want any part of the lawlessness. But the underbelly of society is what keeps the ostensibly upright afloat in today's world, Max knew it and so did his children so they turned a blind eye to his activities. In fact, they both became lawyers and Max IV worked for the DA's office for right now. He had plans of starting his own law firm but he wanted first to make a name for himself outside of his father's, among the attorneys working within the law. Not that the D.A.'s office cared about legalities, it was all about conviction rates. Ilene worked with a firm in downtown Dallas. Her husband, a powerful attorney himself with a prestigious law firm, recommended her for the position. They all knew of Max's dark side but facing reality, it was a means of keeping their ear on the pulse of the criminal element without direct involvement. Max III had worked hand in hand with the Shreveport D.A.'s office on many occasions and had earned a right to exclusion from prosecution. But they'd never had a case on him to start with so it didn't really matter to Max. He just used the D.A.'s office to rid himself of the minor bothersome issues that came with the territory; when that would work in his favor.

In the big city whether it was Dallas or Shreveport, the Periwinkle name carried extreme wight and influence with all sides of the law. All sides, in that the law in the big cities had many shades of gray that most were unaware. Max had his fingers in most of them. The little office front from which he and Ida worked was like a pimple on the face of the mountain underneath. No one really comprehended the extent of his empire as there was no outward appearance of size by the number of people in his operation. All of them were as loyal as Ida because Max had always done right by them, he represented the epitome of all things good while he was doing things that were very, very bad. But bad in the view of who? The ones that allowed him to do his work? Or the ones that gave those people their instructions? The web of intrigue, it boggled the mind; especially as the truth was stranger than fiction.

Lee Roy was being given the chance of a lifetime to enter into a realm most have no clue exists. A realm that lists to the side of the dark but strives to stay in the light while taking advantage of both. In reality, the light was built above the dark in the world of men and the dark was indispensable just as was the foundation of a building, though unseen, it is necessary to keep the building upright and strong. It was not a matter of good and evil as some might express it but it certainly attracted the evil in men's hearts because it was so lucrative. It was a world that was deadly to those that were weak of soul and spirit and perilous to those that were not. But it would exist with or without good people so the good people kept it in check. Very much like politics but without legal protection; which was why Max did is best to stay on the fence between the perceived dark and light.

That night at dinner Max gave Ida the ring he had bought five years earlier hoping that someday she might consider his proposal. Some might think it anti-climactic as he didn't get down on one knee and make a big thing of it and Ida didn't cry out and make a scene. They were both adults and both were happy this day had arrived but it was more of a culmination of having worked to a common goal which had finally been reached. It was no less a happy moment but rather the beginning of a new chapter, a new book in a series, the continuation of what had been established but now with benefits. It was still just as happy as could be expected when Max pulled the box from his pocket and slipped the ring on Ida's finger. They both appreciated what they had together and this was the next logical step.

Ida had not seen the ring previous to this and it was indeed beautiful and larger than she would have imagined even with the generational wealth Max had accumulated. She might have been concerned about wearing it in public but anyone that knew of Max would not even think of robbing her. She would not let herself be caught in a situation that might entice those that didn't know of Max to even consider such a move. It was a valid concern and one that flashed through her mind but at this moment she wasn't going to let that interfere with the joy of the commitment they'd made to each other. It was a commitment and a love born of deep-rooted friendship and long familiarity that had grown warm and closer than anything either of them had ever known. That's why they could both joke about it being just business and know that it was just that and also far, far deeper. Something Max's kids did not necessarily understand about them but were willing to accept due to the long-standing relationship they'd had. It wasn't like she would be taking the place of their mother. It was a whole new life for both Max and Ida.

Regardless of their quiet appreciation for the moment, it did not go unnoticed by the tables surrounding theirs in the restaurant. There was a noticeable uptick in the murmur and the wait staff was immediately aware of the occasion and did not let it slip by. A complimentary bottle of champaign and a small cake with a candle were almost immediately but quietly brought to the table.

Ida joked with Max, "I suppose this means I slept my way to the top?"

"No one can accuse you of that, it's been a ten-year dry season for me and I'm pretty sure for you as well. You have been a bastion of morality as near as I can tell. But the boss likely expects you to start sleeping with him sometime soon."

"I think that can probably be arranged, sometime soon."

They were friends first and it showed in their mutual respect and admiration for each other.

At the office the next morning, Lee Roy was a few minutes early as usual so he couldn't help but notice Ida's new car Max had enticed her to buy was there already but the office was locked. Then he noticed something he'd never seen happen in the year he'd worked with Max and Ida; they pulled up together in one vehicle. Sitting on his scooter smiling like the cheshire cat he couldn't help but laugh out loud as the two exited the vehicle bright red in their faces. There was no denying anything that morning and Lee Roy immediately saw the rock on Ida's finger. He started to whoop and holler but Both Max and Ida shooshed him with their fingers to their lips and Lee Roy about fell over from the response.

"I thought y'all would be shouting it from the roof tops! I could see you were in love almost from the first day I started working for you!"

Ida took charge of the situation and took Lee Roy by the hand, "That's just fine Lee Roy, we appreciate your joy for us but we can talk about his inside." As she led him to the door of the office that Max had just unlocked.

The three of them walked in together and Ida sat Lee Roy down in his usual chair across from hers at her desk. Max stood off to the side smiling and just said, "Thanks Lee Roy, I know you're happy for us and we really appreciate it. We just aren't making a big deal about it because there are some minor changes to the dynamics of our business and that could put Ida at risk from the really bad people out there. She won't even wear her ring most days here at the office because that's like a big red sign over her head saying, Kidnap Me!"

"You think?"

"There is no end to what some would do to take our slice of the pie even though they don't even know how big that slice is. Ida doesn't even know how big it is and I don't share it with her so that she is at less risk. That includes the good guys and the bad guys." Max stopped there and addressed Ida, "What do you think, Ida, is today the day I take him downstairs?"

"You've never taken me downstairs; how would I know?"

"Jealous?"

"A bit."

"Why don't you come with us?"

"That's okay, the less I know, the better. Besides, I need to stay here in case anyone comes in through the front door as opposed to the back door."

Now Lee Roy was curious. He had no idea there was anything more to this operation than Max, Ida and himself. A year he'd been with them and this was the first clue to anything more. Lee Roy followed Max into his office and Max instructed him to close the office door and lock it. Only then did Lee Roy notice the steel bars behind Max's filing cabinet that Max handed to him and instructed him to bar the door as well. One was placed low on the door and one high such that without major effort, no one could force their way in here. Max slid to one side the mirror on the back wall of the tiny office to reveal a door that had otherwise been completely hidden.

"You see, Lee Roy, we have a small front office to limit the number of people and equipment that can be brought in to try and get through my office door. It also makes us look like minnows in a big sea of sharks. Once into my office, one needs to know there is somewhere else to go, you're one of the few that knows that now. Some of my other guys down here know because they've been with me for decades."

Down here meant the stairwell the door behind the mirror he had revealed. "I'm going to introduce you to James, you know each other, you just don't know it yet. He does, you'll get it when you meet him."

At the bottom of the stairwell was another door that Max unlocked and opened, behind that a steel plate and a buzzer button. Max pushed the button that made a bit of a racket and then slid the steel plate to one side. On the other side there were four men with pistols aimed at them which they lowered immediately upon recognizing Max.

"I thought I told you guys, no guns?"

Lee Roy recognized one of the men as the one that had delivered the scooter he'd put to good use.

"Lee Roy, I'd like you to meet James."

James smiled at Max and said, "Guns? What guns?"

Max just shook his head.

"Oh, now I see how it is, keeping it all in the family," said Lee Roy.

"Family is the first to betray you, Lee Roy," said James, "we're just old friends."

"I'm looking forward to being old friends too." Responded Lee Roy.

"How much are we showing him, Max?" Inquired James.

"For now, show him where to come in, where to get his daily shipments and drops, how to come here and how to get to Franky's"

"I'm going to leave you with James today. You'll just have one run today and you can start your regular routines tomorrow again."

"Thanks Mr. Periwinkle!"

"Okay, Lee Roy and mum's the word on what happened this morning."

With that, Max went back out the way he had come in and James took Lee Roy by the arm and guided him through the maze of halls.

"You see this yellow line on the floor? "

"I see six colors of lines on the floor."

"Exactly! You walk only where the yellow lines go. Never on any of the other colors, got it?"

"Why is that?"

"You remember the old line in the old black and white gangster movies, Sleeping With The Fishes?"

"Ya."

"Max likes you, but you'll be sleeping with the fishes anyway if you're caught anywhere but on a yellow line. Got It?"

"I don't have a choice in this, do I?"

"Now I see why Max likes you. Nope, no choice. It's serious business down here and we shoot first, ask questions later."

"Really? You shoot first?"

"No witnesses down here."

"I suppose not."

"So, y'all work in this dungeon all day long?"

"It's a 24 hour a day operation, three shifts. Until you've been with us for a while, you'll never see all of it. "We've only had a very few traitors in the thirty years I've been with Max and no one but Max and I know what happened to them."

"You're kind of harping on this deadly serious thing a little bit."

"I can't impress upon you enough the importance of being faithful to Mr. Periwinkle."

"I feel you, brother."

"Make sure you do."

"So, do I just call you James?"

"We go by first names down here; we all have day jobs and none of us knows where anyone else lives. We are all friends but when we leave here, we are like Baptists at the liquor store. No one knows anyone else."

"Well, that's kind of sad."

"Necessary. Okay, this is where you'll come in."

Without realizing it, Lee Roy found himself in a small street level loading dock area with a garage door open to the outside. There was no visible security force and no door to stop anyone from walking in where Lee Roy had just emerged; but there were cameras and Lee Roy figured they were working and someone was sitting in front of a screen somewhere watching who was coming and who was going.

"You can drive right in here and load up your deliveries and then drop off in this bin right over here."

James showed Lee Roy a drop door just like at the post office. Open it for a parcel, there was no view in. Close it and one might hear the parcel drop out of the bin. It was a slick operation with no way anyone might know what was happening.

"This is your pick-up box on the wall over here," a bin with L.R.P. printed on the front edge.

"You come in, you pick-up, you sign your initials on the clip board hanging beside the bins. Don't forget it, or…"

"Sleeping with the fishes?"

"Max is right, you catch on fast. It's just that simple, do your job, keep your nose clean and no one messes with you."

"It's almost like working for a living."

"It is, but it pays a whole lot better and it's tax free. Just a suggestion, don't go spending your loot around town, you're getting a raise, now that you work under ground. That's what we call this, the underground. You'll be doubling your take but you'll also be doing a lot more. If you mess up, you'll be…"

"Sleeping with the fishes."

"Right again! You can park your Scooter in here next to the wall over on that side when you come in to go to Franky's Do Jo. You will be expected and we will be watching you, always. It never ends, everyone is always under someone's watchful eye. We are worse than the criminals in the IRS. There's an old song,

Every Breath you take,

Every step you take,

Every move you Make,

Oh, can't you see, you belong to me.

I'll be watching you.

It's by the Police, you know that song?"

"Ya."

"Take it to heart."

"You sing it wrong."

"Ya, but I mean every word of it. I think we're going to get along just fine, Lee Roy."

"That's fine by me. You're the boss, James."

They were already down the corridor back on the yellow line and before long they came to a stairwell with a door at the top marked FDJ.

"Do you think you can find your way here come Saturday?"

"Ya, is it okay if I talk to others I meet in the corridors down here?"

"Only for directions. Everyone has a job to do and they're doing it, they don't have time for idle chit chat and neither do you. Besides, that's how we identify narcs. It happens once in a while. I'll walk you back to the loading dock."

James was a man on a mission and had walked fast all morning. There really wasn't much said between them except for what he communicated to Lee Roy. And when they got back to the loading dock it was no different. There was the scooter sitting right where Lee Roy was told to park it, they apparently had a second key, which was only right. James looked at Lee Roy and said, "All right, load up."

"James, just one question."

"Okay, don't waist it, it's your only one for today," he said with a smile.

"Why the underground?"

"Can you imagine all of the attention we'd be getting if we did all of this at street level?"

He turned away and was gone down the corridor.

Lee Roy thought for a moment and he supposed that was true; he wasn't sure what James had meant by all of this, but He figured he'd find out someday. He looked over at his wall bin and saw that it had boxes for him at this point when it had not before; ten of them. Each one with an address type printed on a strip of paper on the side. He loaded them into his scooter trunk and signed them out on the clip board. Lee Roy didn't like having to sign things out but there was a camera that would see him do it so no one would be forging his initials. It was not much different from any warehouse job except that it was illegal and supervision was hidden behind a camera lens. For twenty-four-hundred dollars a week he could live with it; like it or not. And he had no intention of finding out what it was like, sleeping with the fishes.

CHAPTER SEVEN: COMING OF AGE

It had been almost three years ago that Lee Roy had pulled a weapon on Max Periwinkle and indeed, as Max had said, he'd been a punk all that time ago. He came to realize that there were people and forces far greater in the world and even his little tiny town of Shreveport; that were far greater than he'd ever imagined. Greater than the richest of the rich, greater than the banks and greater than any politician. Even Max and his operation, as extensive as he'd come to realize it was, was just a small fish in a great big ocean that didn't care if anyone else got swallowed up. Lee Roy had come to realize that it would take a lifetime for him to come even close to what Max and his predecessors had accomplished if that was even possible in today's world. He'd heeded what James and Max had both encouraged him in not spending his money close to home and in doing so had saved a sizable portion while caring for his mother and sister. He also remembered what Max had once told him about not holding it against his mother if she couldn't hold up her end of the bargain and back sliding in her addiction. And although she had not always succeeded, she had gone into rehab a few times and finally beaten alcohol; she now lived a straight and sober life. He owed a great deal to Max and to Ida as she was the woman that made him feel appreciated and loved while his mother was in recovery.

Most of his instruction in this business had been coming from James and Franky for the past two years although Max never failed to come by and say hello to Lee Roy when he was in the underground at the same time. Lee Roy wondered at how he knew when to come and see him but he imagined the men at the camera screens had instructions to let Max know on occasion. And Lee Roy would stop by at the front office from time to time to see Ida whom he missed a great deal when their daily runs ended and he was relegated to the underground. She always had a smile and a hug for him whenever he stopped in. It amazed him that these people of such wealth and affluence could consider him their equal; and maybe they didn't, but he always felt equal when he was around them. They'd even encouraged him to call them by their first names after a while claiming they were now family.

James left him a note with his pick-up bin one day asking him to come by his office after his drop was completed. That had never happened before; James had always tracked him down and Lee Roy had never known James even had an office. The note merely instructed him to follow the red line. It was almost six in the evening and Lee Roy was tired after having a thirty-five-parcel day. He couldn't complain as his pay steadily went up but that was most of his daylight hours and he was ready for a sit in front of the air conditioner. But he did as requested and followed the red line on the floor past converging and diverging lines of other colors. There was a total of ten colors he counted as he roamed the corridors beneath the city that seemed to go for blocks at a time. But the red line never split although it did converge and seemed to lead only one way. He found himself facing James behind a solid oak desk in well-lit room accompanied by Max and Franky and another man he'd never met.

James invited Lee Roy in and asked him to sit across from the four men which he didn't mind as the room was cooled by its own A.C. unit. Max addressed him first and thanked him for living up to his end of the bargain and doing a stellar job for them. He was followed by Franky who recited his accomplishments at the Do Jo. Then James chimed in and told him that he was no longer needed as a runner for the shipping dock. Lee Roy was stunned; this was not what he had expected after nearly three years of faithful work. Then all four men burst into laughter and it dawned on Lee Roy that he'd been had. He wasn't quite sure where this was going but he felt a wave of relief wash over him even in his traumatized state of disbelief. Max addressed him again, "We have been grooming your replacement."

Again, Lee Roy was confused.

"You are turning eighteen next month and you will be an adult and as a runner, you become a liability to yourself and to our operation. You are getting a promotion," continued James.

The three Laughed again.

"A promotion?"

"Yes, you will be running one of our cassinos as an assistant manager, if you accept, It's just down the road a piece."

"Oh, you guys think you got jokes?"

"It's for real, Lee Roy." Said Franky, "We have to replace you as a runner but you've proven yourself loyal and trustworthy so we want you to stay with us and help run the Golden Oyster Cassino."

Lee Roy sat for a moment trying to take it all in. "I don't know nothing about no cassino!"

"No, you don't, but you will in a month's time," said James, "I'd like you to meet Jean Baptist. He is the manager and part owner of The Golden Oyster. He's named after the founder of New Orleans and he runs a tight ship."

Lee Roy stood to shake Jean's hand, Jean returned the respect of standing and accepted Lee Roy's hand. "It is a pleasure to make your acquaintance, Lee Roy."

"You as well, my brother from another mother."

The men chuckled at Lee Roy's attempt to endear himself to Jean.

It was not lost on Jean either. Jean handed him his business card and told him not to lose it.

"That is almost a get out of jail free card in a pinch. 'Almost' being the key word so try not to need it."

"Yes, sir."

"That's very nice of you but we need to get past the sir part right now. I appreciate the respect but we will be best friends before long or you will be…"

All five men said it together, "Sleeping with the fishes."

With that James poured a drink for each of them and they sat there and discussed what would be expected in the coming month. Franky excused himself shortly as he had a class at the Do Jo but the four others sat for almost an hour going over some of the responsibilities and all of the expectations; of which there were so very many.

Jean finally asked, "Are you ready to step up to this challenge?"

Lee Roy answered with enthusiasm, "Ready? I was born for this! Just one question, the last assistant, is he…"

"Sleeping with the fishes!" the men nodded and said in a subdued voice.

"Ya? Well don't do that to me, okay? I'll come back and I'll haunt your asses!"

Jean Baptist said, "Be at the Oyster at noon tomorrow. You will make more money than god but you will work the hours that he sleeps."

The men laughed and shook hands and the three remaining elder men watched as Lee Roy walked down the corridor to retrieve his scooter and head home.

Max broke the silence first, "What's your opinion, gentlemen?"

The other two nodded in the affirmative. They poured another drink, closed the door and shot the shit for another hour.

Lee Roy knew right where the Oyster was and showed up right at noon as instructed. He was escorted in to see Jean, walking past some very incredulous faces of security and dealers. He walked past with confidence as Franky had trained him well and he had no doubt he could hold his own with most of these folks. But there was a look of challenge in the eyes of some of them and it might be a tough row to hoe. Everyone knew the new assistant manager was coming in that day but they were not expecting someone so young. It was obvious to Lee Roy he'd need to prove himself to this crew but he wasn't sure what it might take. He'd just have to wait and see what the challenges would be. He hoped he could meet those challenges as might Max or Ida with poise, grace and charm but he suspected he might need to meet one or two with a succinct response as might Franky; He was almost hoping for the second as that would put a definitive end to wrongful speculation on the part of underlings. It just wouldn't gain any loyalty points; and he was smart enough to know he would need those in a supervisory role. Especially with as big as some of these security personnel were; freaks of nature!

He imagined himself as a young Wesley Snipes Character in Blade walking amongst the vampires fresh out of wooden stakes. His armed security brought him to a door that read, Mr. Baptist and next to it was another door that read, Mr. Pope. That was Lee Roy's last name! They must have been planning this for a day or two now. That rather boosted his confidence. He smiled as he thought to himself, they were Pope and the Baptist. Even he gagged a bit at the pun, but hey, it worked. He hoped it would go smoothly but he was ready for the necessary work involved and an expected bumpy first couple of months. One of his escorts knocked on Jean's door and he heard the word, "Come," from within. The security guard opened the door for him and as he walked past, he thought he caught a sneer from the man.

Jean stood and offered his hand to Lee Roy. "Welcome my friend, I see you found us."
"No problem, Mr. Baptist. It's good to see you again."
"The pleasure is all mine. Please, call me Jean if you wish, I only ask that we both refer to each other by last names out on the floor when we are working. It promotes a more formal environment there, but in here, we are family and friends."
"Thank you, Jean."

Lee Roy felt he would be very happy working with Jean; and for the next week he was engulfed in a process that was obviously designed to immerse him in the accounting of the immense money laundering that goes on in casinos. Jean assured him he would never need to do this as part of his job but that he needed to learn it to know the foundational principles of the business. He had people that did this full time but Jean wanted Lee Roy to know it in case there was ever a need to be involved legally. It wasn't likely but it was just another level of understanding and protection for the organization. During this first week, Jean was with Lee Roy almost constantly except when he was needed on the floor and even then, he would sometimes drag Lee Roy around with him as this would be his job also in the all too near future. It was a lot to take in but being together so much allowed the two men to get to know each other. It also showed the other employees a solidarity between the two that would support Lee Roy's authority; a necessary element to leading everyone by example.

As Lee Roy appeared beside Jean more and more it seemed to him the original tensions caused by his presence were diminishing and he felt more comfortable in addressing the staff when Mr. Baptist asked for his input. That also signaled the staff that his opinion counted to Mr. Baptist and that his word was gold in nearly all situations. Only on rare occasion did Jean modify anything that Lee Roy instructed and it was generally something minor. Most often Jean would wait until they were out of earshot of those involved and then he would give his critique. It helped make Lee Roy look more in tune with things than he himself actually felt and it also bolstered confidence in how he instructed the staff; both to the staff and to himself. Even Lee Roy had not realized how much Max, James and Franky had influenced his thinking and his capability to deal with people. But it was shining through now that he had to do it on a daily basis. Most all of his concerns about how the staff perceived him had melted away by the time he was to take over the day shift. Jean had sent him one day his first week there, to be fitted for a suit, by the third week seven suites were delivered matching those of Jean and the rest of the male staff. Jean smiled when he told him, "Don't outgrow those." But Lee Roy suspected that was good advice as opposed to a joke of some kind.

Day shift was the slow shift in the business and Lee Roy felt prepared to face it by himself when that time came. And it came faster than he ever expected. The transition went as smoothly as could be expected and having been there a month already he knew most of the staff by their first names. Those he didn't know he would speak to on their breaks if they were willing and got to know them. Lee Roy made a point of being everyone's friend first and boss second but he never allowed one to interfere with the other as far as his duties were concerned. He hoped that would avoid any real issues with most people and it worked well for him. Even the big burly security guard that had sneered at him in the beginning warmed up to him and gave a slight bow whenever addressing him as Mr. Pope. Lee Roy was kind of fond of Big John as everyone called him. He was more of a big teddy bear than one would ever suspect. Most of what Lee Roy did was scheduling shifts as many of his flock had two or more jobs, baby sitters, school issues and needed his help juggling them. Then on payday, many of the night staff came in to get their checks along with handing them out to his own shift. On those days he seldom left his office.

On Occasion Max would stop in and have a meeting with the managers and their assistants. Lee Roy always enjoyed those days, especially on the rare occasion Ida came with him. She generally excused herself from the meetings because she wanted plausible deniability and Lee Roy would track her down as she visited with the female staff. He really liked to have a little time catching up with her. On his rare day off he would go by the office and visit if they had the time which they almost always did. They were indeed, a family of sorts. It's true what he'd heard about an organization reflecting from the top down what the owner was like as his people were generally a reflection of him. Most everyone at the cassino were like family as well. There were always a few outliers in such a large organization but they all did their best to help each other. No one would suspect the criminality that flowed under the streets in the underground.

Life was good for Lee Roy, his sister and their mother. Of course, He had to buy a vehicle when he went to work at the casino, he couldn't be seen riding a scooter into work and besides, his replacement needed that to do his job for Max. Lee Roy had bought a sweet little Toyota Camry for his sister and mother and he bought something more to the stylings of his new job for himself; a Toyota Avalon. He paid cash which raised some eyebrows and even prompted the local yokals to stakeout his house for a week to find out where he was getting his money. Just because he loved his new position in life and to really mess with their heads, he left one day early for work, picked up a half dozen box of donuts and walked up to their car and knocked on the window. Classic Eddie Murphy stuff right there. Handing them his business card he invited them to come over to the casino sometime soon and he'd comp their drinks. They drove off without a word. And he stood in the street laughing and pointing at them in their rear-view mirror, the one finger raised to the sky pointing if you know the code; you're number one! His momma scolded him for that one and he couldn't help himself but to relate it to the guys at work. He was an instant hero. Momma and his sister enjoyed the donuts.

And so, his days were filled with the mundane, the problems of employees and the occasional rowdy customer or card counter that Security regularly handled. He knew the books were being cooked in the back room but he had no overt knowledge of such things and he didn't care to know. At one point Jean called him into the video surveillance room to point out some suspicious characters from the night shift. He asked if the day shift had noted them of which Lee Roy had no knowledge. Jean asked him to make the day shift monitors aware of the assumed feds and to review the tapes for a week back. Lee Roy made that happen.

Sure enough, they were being cased by either the feds or someone looking to make a hit on the money room; these days that might be the feds as well. Once all the culprits had been positively identified, Jean let Lee Roy know it was time to take them all down at the same time. Funny thing about an operation of the type they were observing was that they were also working shifts that overlapped to make their observations. Just like cops sitting on a stake out, one crew didn't leave until the next one was in position; so, this would be a quick sweep and disposal of a nuisance. Lee Roy was in charge but his people were the ones that knew what to do. He would be a professional witness to what they had observed and what they would be doing about it. He made sure they had enough footage from the day shift to document the existence of the observers and got the DVRs backed up to Blu-rays which he put into the safe.

When the hour came to hit these guys both he and Jean ensured the DVRs were shut down. System power failure, the entire casino would suffer a momentary power interruption and the DVRs would take a moment to come back up. A manufactured moment timed to cover their butts. As soon as that moment came, the power mains were flipped off and then flipped back on which was the signal for security to grab these guys two on one and cuff them and remove them to a room under the casino. There was so much confusion from the power and the resulting attack on these observers that the entire place was in shock. Dealers, servers and customers all froze in place while security and these intruders struggled, were subdued and disappeared through various doors around the main room. It took all of forty seconds to complete the exercise and it was over without a trace of it ever occurring. The DVRs came back up and all the customers were comped a drink for their inconvenience. No one was the wiser. It didn't even make the papers.

Because Security was busy with the intruders Jean and Lee Roy both took position on the floor to keep an eye on things. It appeared they'd gotten all of the people they had been watching and a security guard surfaced to give Jean a report about fifteen minutes later, then disappeared through a door again. Jean casually walked over and spoke low into Lee Roy's ear that the feds would be storming the place soon, maybe about an hour, to try and find their missing men. Security had identified them as FBI and that meant trouble. They probably wouldn't be able to get a warrant in that time but they'd try to bully their way around. To be prepared to know nothing and reveal even less. The staff already knew to keep their mouths shut, even any noobs knew the score. When the feds arrived it was in force but security had already started wandering back in after finishing whatever it was they were doing. Jean motioned Lee Roy to stay at his side when the rush began. The Oyster was operating full tilt at the time and the rush of the feds caused business to come to a screeching halt as many of the customers suddenly remembered they had to be elsewhere.

A man that took himself to be very important walked up to Jean and Lee Roy; he knew exactly to whom he was speaking and addressed them by their first names. He had two men with him that Lee Roy recognized immediately as the ones that were bird dogging him at this home. When special agent Rogers introduced himself along with special agents Clovis and Patterson Lee Roy couldn't help himself but make the correction that he and Jean were Mr. Baptists and Mr. Pope. Just for good measure he questioned, "And you two gentlemen again? Was that special agents, Clitoris and Peckerwood?"
Jean smiled and put his hand in front of Lee Roy as the two agents puffed up in defiance of the mocking. And said, "Come now Mr. Pope, we don't want to ruffle any chicken feathers, we are all friends here."

That set the tone for the moment and special Agent Rogers knew he was getting nowhere without a warrant this evening.

"I'm missing several men that were stationed in here to observe your operation, I suppose I'm not going to find them tonight?"

Jean answered, "Whatever do you mean, special Agent Rogers? We didn't notice anyone loitering this afternoon. You are welcome to look around if you'd like."

The other special agents that had come in with the rush on the Oyster were milling around trying to ask question of the staff and customers to no avail; no one knew anything.

Rogers motioned to his men to spread out and look around but ten minutes later he approached Jean and Lee Roy again and asked, "What's behind the doors along the wall?"

"That's where we keep our accounting staff, the safe, employee lockers and various other business aspects of the casino."

"I can just imagine. I'll be back tomorrow with a warrant. You'd better hope my men find their ways home and that I don't find anything implicating you and your people. It will be a blood bath."

"It already has been," said Jean with a wicked little grin.

Rogers hesitated knowing full well there was meaning behind the remark, but not knowing exactly what, he walked away.

As he did Jean turned to Lee Roy, "Seriously Mr. Pope? Clitoris and Peckerwood?"

"You liked that, didn't you?"

"Yes, but DAMN that was bold on your first raid."

They walked back to their offices to where Big John was waiting on them.

"Everything is as expected, Mr. Baptist."

"Very Good, John. Everything is sprayed down with bleach?"

"Yes, Mr. Baptist."

"And the fish?"

"They'll sleep with full stomachs tonight."

Lee Roy was stunned by that exchange; he was not expecting the part about the fish.

So, that wasn't just what they said around here for humor.

"Two words you need to know but never speak, Mr. Pope. Wood chipper. We learned long ago that if we deal harshly and immediately with our problems, they tend to go away permanently. And the rumors also keep the staff in line."

"Well, that would tend do it," replied Lee Roy.

"Yes, Mr. Pope. It certainly does."

"The best part is when they go in feet first."

Lee Roy turned to Jean with a look of shock on his face.

"You heard it here first, Lee Roy."

And Jean said it so nonchalantly.

The next morning Rogers, Clitoris and Peckerwood arrived at Nine a.m. with a warrant and a dozen agents but the door to the disposal room was well hidden and they never even found it much less asked to open it. Strangely, their men for whom they were looking never arrived home and the families and neighbors all knew they would never be seen again. Sadly, for them, not so much for the casino. It was a harsh world but it kept things on an even keel and the feds seldom tried to raid them because of the community pressure to keep family pain to a minimum. Everyone knew and every one feared when some go-getter would go and get their husbands, sons and fathers 'disappeared' as they would say. They knew it was more a sure thing than being Clintoned.

After the morning rousting, the casino was like a grave yard, in more ways than one, but by noon things started to pick up again. Jean had come in for the serving of the warrant but excused himself to go and get some sleep before it was his turn to come back in. Like it or not, it was a regular job with regular hours to be fulfilled and they all had to do their part. He went up to one of the suites and came back at his leisure. One of the advantages of being the top dog. Lee Roy was having more fun than being worried about the legal aspect. He couldn't help himself but laugh every time Clitoris and Peckerwood showed their faces inside the establishment and their obvious discomfort and even vile hatred of him was like adding fuel to his fire. It was to a point that even the staff was enjoying the nick names and greeting them as such when they made their slowly decreasing visits. Lee Roy wasn't sure how the agents could even show their faces. Jean had mentioned that he should lighten up a bit and of course he agreed; but they both knew that wasn't going to happen.

After that, the harassment stopped but from time-to-time Lee Roy saw his agency friends around town checking him out or sitting well away down the street from his mother's place. He had often thought about getting his own home but he felt more inclined to stay close to his family now that the feds had so much interest in watching them all. All Jean had to say was, "One gets used to it."

At that point there were no more stake outs within the casino although the staff occasionally reported seeing suspected agents in close proximity to the entrance. By this time though the mass extinction event of agents had been well digested, so to speak, and no amount of investigation would or even could expose what had actually happened. The trail had gone cold and no one could question Lee Roy's capability to provide for his mother and sister. He even filed impressive tax returns that the IRS forensic accounting teams were unable to debunk. Tax and accounting applications on his home computer kept Lee Roy on the straight and narrow and he seldom paid more than ten percent in any given year.

One evening when Lee Roy felt like visiting with Max and Ida, they both happened to be at the front office at the same time and he broached the subject with Max; Ida excusing herself when she realized. Lee Roy had brought some very expensive whiskey to share and Max felt a bit talkative. Lee Roy asked if Max had this vision when they had first met?

"No, I never trust a person that far ahead. But you seemed different to me and you had a spark in your eye, a hunger and a reason that was driving you. I felt you could be nurtured."

"You sure took a big chance on me Max. I don't know if I've ever expressed how much I appreciate what you've done for me and my family; but it made a difference that I can never repay."

"That's all right, son." Max had taken to calling Lee Roy, son. "Your services paid me well for taking a chance on you and I've enjoyed having you as part of the organization. Someday I hope you will pay it forward. Jean tells me you are relentless on the feds?"

Laughing, Lee Roy admitted, "Ya, I give them a lot to think about while they sit down the street finding out nothing about me and my peeps."

"I notice you don't seem to like girls?" a wry smile coming across his face.

"Come on Max, you should know me better than that. I just ain't found no one that respects me like Ida Respects you."

Max was taken back a bit by that. He wasn't expecting to have had that kind of effect on Lee Roy. He was happy though; Lee Roy just wasn't anything like the young man he'd confronted on the street that first day so many years ago. The changes were deep and profound and Max was happy that Lee Roy had found a better life in what Max had been able to offer him.

"I'm glad that you find our relationship inspirational, Lee Roy."

"Shoot Max, everyone could take a page or two, even a chapter out of you and Ida's playbook."

"Well, thank you son. I hope it serves you well. We have enjoyed you immensely as well."

They sat and talked for a while and Max called Ida back in as her work day was finished and she should be a part of the conversation. It was always an enjoyable time for them as well as Lee Roy when they all three got the chance to visit.

Even Ida partook of the whisky that day as she normally abstained but a couple of hours flew by as the three of them talked and laughed more than they had in many months. It was getting late and the three friends were all starting to yawn, as much from the whisky as from the hour and hugging, they parted ways still laughing as they each waved goodbye and climbed into their respective vehicles. He didn't say anything to Max but Max noticed Lee Roy's gaze up the street behind Max's back. He turned to see the feds just a block up on the other side sitting in a company car watching them.

"Best go home and leave that alone, son."

"I know Max, it's just so tempting."

"Now, don't go there."

Realizing about what the two were speaking Ida turned and saw the agents behind their car.

"Come on, Max. Let's get out of here."

"Go straight home, Lee Roy."

"I will, Max."

Lee Roy was thinking that Agents Clitoris and Peckerwood were getting a bit bold and as he drove home with the twins following him; he began to hatch a plan. He had to give them a reason to never want to follow his family ever again but it would need to be a permanent fix. He would talk with Jean when he came in tomorrow but he was thinking Big John and a few of the boys would need to be involved. He wanted to see the wood chipper do its job as well. It wasn't right that these two were beginning to affect him and his friends and family. None of them had ever done a thing to deserve this type of harassment and it was high time it stopped. For now, he simply wanted to relax and have one more drink before bed. He was careful not to keep too much liquor in the house and only in the drawer in his room. He put the half pint bottle into the vest pocket of his jacket when he parked, when he looked up, he saw Clitoris and Peckerwood's car parked blocking him in and they weren't in it. This was new.

His door was thrown open and Peckerwood grabbed him by the arm and started pulling him out. It was barely dark and the lights in the house came on and that distracted Peckerwood for the moment that Lee Row needed to get the drop on him.

His foot came down on the arch in Peckerwoods foot as his elbow came up under his chin and at the same time, he was able to stand out of his seat and the fingers of his right hand jammed into the eyes of the agent. Clitoris was right there but just not quickly enough. Franky had taught Lee Roy all the dirtiest moves and that strength, although helpful had nothing on speed and accuracy. Peckerwood wasn't going to hurt him anymore tonight so he looked right under Clitoris' chin and throat punched him, then a knee to the groin. While Clitoris was incapacitated, he stepped around back of Peckerwood and put him in a sleeper. It was only fifteen seconds and he was out like a light. And then it was Clitoris' turn to go to sleep. Both men pissed their pants.

By that time his little sister Angelique had stepped out on the porch and was screaming for help from momma and the neighbors. But Lee Roy didn't need it. In fact, he had to tell her to be quiet. It was best if there were no witnesses for the next part. Lee Roy popped the deck lid and threw both men into the trunk, it took only a few seconds and he had it closed again. By that time the next-door neighbor had stuck her head out. Lee Roy just looked at Mrs. Jones, put his finger to his lips and shook his head no. She nodded, went back inside and quietly closed her door.

"I got this, Angelique; go check their car. Are the keys in the ignition?" Angelique nodded. "Go get your gloves on and drive it down two blocks and leave it there with the keys in it and the windows open."

Angelique ran back inside, Momma stuck her head out the door, "You okay Lee Roy?"

It's going to be okay, Momma." I'll come home later and tell you all about it."

"All right Lee Roy, you just be careful."

"Yes, momma, you know I will."

With that Angelique was back outside and already driving the Agent's car down the street. By the time she was walking back to the house Lee Roy was on his way down the road with his

window down he told her, "Thanks, Baby girl."
She smiled and waved at him. He smiled, she knew the score and would back him up any day of the week and twice on Sundays.

He got on the phone to Jean and told him what had happened. Jean and Big John would meet him at the back door with muscle to enforce the situation; Lee Roy only had to get there without being stopped by the po-po. That shouldn't be an issue, Lee Roy had a near perfect driving record and most of the town's cops knew him by his philanthropic donations to children's charities supported by the cop shops around town. Nobody else had ever messed with him. By the time he got to the back door of the Oyster he could hear the two men making a ruckus in his trunk and it was loud. Jean and Big John had the back door open with eight other men standing there. Clitoris and Peckerwood barely had a moment to realize where they were when the contingency had beat them into unconsciousness again and dragged them inside. Jean instructed one of the men standing there to get the interior out of the trunk and then told Lee Roy to go to the next town over in the morning and purchase new material for the trunk. They wouldn't likely have it in stock so his vehicle would need to be 'in the shop' until it arrived and he could have it put in. "Get yourself a rental from the dealership."

Jean told Lee Roy to go home and get some sleep, this part of the problem wasn't something for which he was ready to deal. Lee Roy was disappointed but he knew Jean was only looking out for his psychological wellbeing. He had been looking forward to that drink before bed and he thought it would be nice to get the thoughts out of his head and his adrenaline back to normal. He could still feel his heart beating a bit fast. It was easy to say yes to Jean as he always seemed to have a handle on everything, calm level headed and almost fatherly, Lee Roy had developed a deep respect for the man he now called his friend.

His drive home was uneventful and when he got there, Momma just looked him over to be sure he wasn't hurt. Angelique had already told her nearly all the details as she'd seen most of it. He stopped by Mrs. Jone's place before going in his own door and gave her a bouquet of flowers he'd picked up at the neighborhood bodega and thanked her for her cooperation for which she smiled and told him he was such a sweet boy to take such good care of his momma and sister. He knew she would not be a problem. The agents' car was already gone and Lee Roy didn't care where, it wasn't even a memory at this point. He went to his room and poured himself a double and turned on the news; he was asleep before he had finished his drink.

The alarm came early the next morning but Lee Roy didn't mind. He was rather wondering how things had gone after he left the Oyster but he knew he wouldn't likely learn anything until the afternoon when Jean was due in for his shift. He greeted his momma and Angelique who had some toast and coffee ready for him when he walked into the kitchen. Angelique was not his sister's real name. She preferred it over her real name of Bobby Jo; and in fact, she was a beautiful young lady and Angelique was more fitting to her beauty and personality. Lee Roy kissed his momma and hugged his siter goodbye and left for this incredible adventure he called his job.

First, he had to stop over at the Toyota dealership in the town of Haughton. He gave a call into work and let the night shift manager know he'd be an hour late. That was okay by him, he'd already heard what happened the night before and knew Lee Roy needed to make the trip out of town. When Lee Roy walked into work, he couldn't help noticing that all eyes were on him. He felt like a celebrity as several of the security walked up to him and shook his hand and the servers all seemed to be whispering to each other. It was over almost as soon as it had begun but it seemed he'd made the necessary impression he'd worried about when he first got the job. No one needed to challenge or be challenged and he had the reputation that was needed in his position to support his somewhat diminutive size. He went and found the night manager and let him know he could go home but Sean wanted to know the details first. Lee Roy couldn't help but tell him of the fight and how he'd dispatched the two before they even knew they'd lost the fight. His response was one of admiration and he finally went home when all of his questions had been satiated. After that, the day was just another day but it seemed to Lee Roy that several of his staff seemed a bit more reverent in his presence. When Jean came in, he asked Lee Roy into his office.

"Max and I spoke last night already and it seems you had no choice in what you did. He said to assure you that you had done exactly what you needed to do. He said just ride low and in the middle of the pack for now and see if this blows over. Not likely, it's the second time agents have gone missing in a manner associated with the Oyster but we aren't going to stir the pot at all until they make us do so. We expect Rogers to get another warrant and we have the disposal room sealed off and covered up already so it is not just hidden, it appears to be gone. They will likely get a warrant for your home as well. Are you prepared?"
"I had never even thought about it. I don't think there's anything there they can use."
"Call home now, right now, use my phone and let them know to expect a search."
Lee Roy did so and Angelique and his momma had already thought of that but they lived clean and sober but for his little bottle he left on the night stand the night before. They'd already cleaned that up.

Lee Roy sure wanted to see this disposal room but it seemed this was not the time to ask. They must have gone to some heroic extent to make it disappear overnight.
"Did the agents' car disappear?"
"Before I even got home last night."
"Good, you had a moment of brilliance with that. Any time we can make things happen by someone else's hand it's a good

move. You don't have any marks from the fight, do you?"

"Momma looked me over last night but why don't you go ahead and take peak to be sure in your own mind."

"Thanks, I'll do that."

Lee Roy stood and took off his jacket and let Jean look him over.

"You look good."

Most of the day had already gone by so they did not expect the police to raid them yet. First, they had to convince a judge there was some basis for the warrants necessary. Some judge was obviously looking to close them down and he'd probably sign off on just about anything at this point but it had to at least look legal.

"Okay, go home for the night and tomorrow, business as usual?"

"Sounds good, Jean."

"Okay, don't be surprised if they come into your home tonight, it's what they like to do."

"I'll warn momma and Angelique."

"Okay, sleep well, if they let you."

It was almost as if this was just another day except for the little things going on in the background and Lee Roy was left shaking his head over the whole thing. Lee Roy was home before dark and Momma and Angelique both were full of questions about his day. They had a good conversation over a dinner of spaghetti, boiled okra and hot buttered corn bread. His family had not noticed anyone strange in the neighborhood and it seemed nothing would come of this. But they all agreed to stay vigilant as the feds were not known to just give up once they had their noses to the ground; hounds that they were known to be. Lee Roy made sure momma and Angelique understood the feds were likely to come in in the middle of the night as that was their style to harass and catch unaware when they wanted maximum embarrassment, even shame for the victims of their ire. Often times they didn't even care if it was legal, they just wanted to make an example of people that didn't conform to their system.

Lee Roy barely slept that night expecting any moment for the front door to be kicked in and have guns pointed in their faces, that would be the way of the FBI. He normally slept in the raw but tonight he dawned a pair of boxer shorts, just in case. He was not wrong to take precautions but for whatever reason, tonight was not the night. He hoped they might get away lucky on this one but experience and wisdom told him otherwise. He'd seen to many acquaintances homes fairly destroyed by federal searches and he did not expect to be treated any differently when, not if the time came. They had nothing for which to be arrested unless the feds planted evidence and Lee Roy new for a fact they were not above doing so. Corruption ran deep in the federal government and anyone with a brain was aware of that fact.

When morning finally raised its eyes above the horizon Lee Roy had only just gone to sleep. Momma and Angelique had not had a good night either and they all sat at the kitchen table in silence drinking coffee and eating buttered toast with strawberry jam. Lee Roy expressed the thought the feds might be waiting to yield maximum effect upon executing a warrant or possibly they had hit other locations last night. Either way he warned his momma and sister to be on the alert for strangers and to give him a call immediately if they noticed any rats scurrying around the hood. He left for work at the regular time, he was like clockwork that way and he almost hated that fact. It made him too predictable and that was never a good thing when it came to being intercepted.

The drive into The Golden Oyster was uneventful but for the fact that he knew he had a tail the entire drive. A patrol car had dropped in behind him as he turned the corner out of his neighborhood and stayed there until he was within a block of the casino. It was an obvious ploy to shake him up and although he didn't like it, he couldn't help but wonder if that was the best they could do; it wasn't even a federal vehicle but one of the locals. Before he even got out of his Avalon, he called home to check on Momma and Angelique. They reported nothing out of the ordinary so Lee Roy was wondering why the tail coming into work? Was it coincidence? In his experience there was no such thing as coincidence. He felt like the mouse in a game of cat and mouse and that did not sit well with him. He was accustomed to being the cat. Maybe too much so. He had his morning chat with Sean who seemed a bit subdued this morning but otherwise all was well. Just the normal scheduling snafu's trying to help the servers and dealers stay happy in their convoluted family needs.

That's when all hell broke loose and every door alarm in the place sounded with people screaming, glass breaking and men shouting. It was a full-scale invasion of feds into the building form every point of entry or exit.

Sean shouted, "Damn those bastards!" He dialed Max's number and yelled, "They're here!" Just as Special Agent Rogers walked in and slapped the phone from his hand. It hit the desk and broke. They slammed both men over the office desk and cuffed their hands behind them. When they stood them up again Lee Roy smiled and said, "Well, hi there Rogers Rabbit! How's Jessica doing? So good of you to grace us with your ugly face again!"

Rogers slugged him across the chin, "Take them in and read them their rights."

Lee Roy laughed, "Oh, you mean like we have the right to be assaulted?"

One of the goons with Rogers shoved Lee Roy through the doorway slamming his shoulder on the door jam. He and Sean were put in separate vehicles and taken into FBI headquarters where they could only assume the feds were trying desperately to find anything they could at the casino for which to hold them. An hour later Max and his attorneys were right there getting the two out on grounds of insufficient evidence and falsifying a warrant. The attorneys guaranteed there would be charges filed and Lee Roy did not doubt it. The suits these guys wore said they made enough money that they were not to be trifled with.

Max shook their hands as they came out the from FBI headquarters and looked at Lee Roy, "Rogers Rabbit? Really?"

Lee Roy laughed and said, "I just said what the voices in my head told me to say."

Max laughed at that. He asked, "Have you seen that man's wife? She is Jessica rabbit. I don't know how a guy that looks like that ever got a woman that looks like her."

"No shit?"

"No shit."

In twenty minutes, they were back at the casino with the attorneys while the staff cleaned up the mess from being rousted. They'd made sure to do the maximum amount of damage they might get away with legally but the attorneys insisted on a complete inventory of everything that had been broken; including a couple of roulette tables. They would be suing over this flagrant abuse of power.

Lee Roy called home again and found that everything was alright. He was becoming more and more concerned with this new aggression from the feds as were Max and Sean. It should have ended after the first loss of agents, wasn't that enough of a warning? What did they expect? Trying to beat a guy in his own driveway, of course there would be retaliation. But to retaliate against the retaliation was a war and the feds would lose a war. At least he assumed they would lose from what he'd seen happen so far. If they continued, they would quickly run out of agents and the fish would be fat and sassy.

Sean excused himself to go home and get some sleep and Max sat down with Lee Roy after the attorneys had departed. "I don't mean to be accusatory, Lee Roy, but this seems to have started when you started calling Agents Clovis and Patterson, Clitoris and Peckerwood."

"What is this, second grade? Sticks and stones can break my bones, Max. I have to say that maybe I pissed in someone's Wheaties, but I have to think there's something even bigger behind all this. Didn't you have some kind of an unspoken truce going on here?"

"We sure saw it that way. We didn't bother them as long as they didn't bother us. If they were going to start something I'd expect it to be with the underground. But maybe they still don't know much about that; even after all these years."

"I got to address the elephant in the room, Max. I am your only black manager in all the operations I know about."

Max nodded his head, Lee Roy was right about that, "Yes, but I just can't imagine that being the only reason in this day and age. It's not the 50's and there has been plenty of advancement of blacks throughout the community in every respect. I'll put out some feelers and see what I can find out."

With that, Max rose and offered Lee Roy his hand then turned to leave. "Oh, one more thing Lee Roy, make doubly sure you have nothing in your home they can bring against you."

"Already done Max. In my last call home, a bit ago I asked Angelique to put in a call to a security company we looked at. They'll be wiring us up this afternoon."

"I'm sure that's wise, cameras inside as well as out, I hope?"

"Yes, sir. Wired for sight and sound."

"Good, good. Well, enjoy the rest of your day."

"As soon as I put some super glue on my jaw to keep it in place. That little coney can swing!"

Max took a second look at Lee Roy as he'd not expected him to know the word, coney. Max hadn't heard it for a month of blood moons and had not thought about it for at least that long. Lee Roy laughed as he knew exactly what was going through Max's head, "I read The Hobbit when I was young."

Max, smiled and nodded understanding, then continued out of the office.

Now Lee Roy could take care of his people's needs. They had all been very patient and he knew there would be questions and concerns that required his attention. After all, these were the people that kept the customers happy so that they could take their money with a smile and pay Lee Roy his insanely huge salary. They were the back bone of the casino and he was well aware of their importance. Unlike other owners, Max, James and Franky respected their people and that's why everyone was so extremely loyal. When it came to defending each other, they were all family like no other family might ever be. They were as thick as thieves as that's exactly what they were and they made no bones about it. About that time Lee Roy's revery was interrupted as Katey Sherwood needed the afternoon off to pick up her sick three-year-old from day care. How could he refuse? "I'll bring him in to finish my shift. I can't afford to lose the money."

"Don't you bring no sick child in here! You take the afternoon off and make arrangements for his care before your next shift. I won't dock your pay for today."

Katey was ecstatic, "Thank you, Mr. Pope!" and she promised to get it taken care of.

This assistant manager stuff was easy if he imagined himself in the position of the worker with which he was dealing and he knew Katey wasn't making enough money to make ends meet at times.

When Lee Roy's shift was over Jean came into his office and greeted him wondering how he enjoyed his short incarceration. Word travels fast.

"My butt's still tight if that's what you're asking? Why, you interested?"

Jean just howled at that. Lee Roy was quick witted but sometimes he was just downright shocking.

"No, my friend, although I'm happy to know you're still intact. I was afraid you'd need some hemorrhoid cream or even a surgeon."

"Naw, I kept Sean at arm's distance."

"You settle down now, I'll be telling him you said that."

"Don't you dare! He'll be wanting some of this fine stuff."

"No, really, everything good?"

"Ya, little Rogers Rabbit clocked me but Max's attorneys are going to file charges on him. Maybe that will cool his jets."

"Let's hope so. We don't need any more of this notoriety. Business is off almost ten percent since this started."

"That's a chunk of change. You think that's what they are trying to do? Shut us down?"

"It's hard to say. It might just be a side effect of their primary intention. I'm sure it would make them happy if they knew"

"I got to get out of here, having a security system installed this afternoon. I want to see everything before they finish and leave."

"All right, Lee Roy. You have a good night."

"Thank you, Mr. Baptist. It's always a pleasure."

"The pleasure is all mine, Mr. Pope."

Lee Roy got out to his car but not before noticing a patrol car down the street and the officer inside watching him specifically. He could only assume at this point that the Feds and the locals were in cahoots and it appeared the locals were watching his schedule. He got back out of his car and went to find Jean and asked him to walk out with him. On the way out, Lee Roy asked if the locals had been following him around and he hadn't noticed that. Lee Roy said, "Follow my lead, we're going to give this guy a reason to go home and change his shorts." He started walking toward the car with Jean in tow. That got the officer's attention real fast; most people weren't that bold. They could see him sit up in the seat and his seat belt came off in case he needed to get out of the car. Lee Roy called out, "Hi Mr. officer! What you doing following me around?"

There was no response. Jean liked this game and he piped in, "Is there something we can do for you Mr. Officer?"

The officer opened his door stepped out and stood at the ready. Lee Roy stepped right up beside the man and Jean fell in on the other side. The officer stepped away which put Lee Roy and Jean between him and his cruiser. He was obviously nervous with his hand on his service weapon. Lee Roy took note of his name tag that said Prince and his collar pin insignia (TPR) denoted trooper and the game was afoot.

"Hi there, Trooper Princes." Said Lee Roy offering his hand to the officer. At the same time Jean did exactly as had Lee Roy and even stepped in a bit on the officer, "I'm Jean Baptist, Trooper Princes." Trooper Princes called for backup and the guys laughed at him, "What's the matter Trooper Princes? We thought you just wanted to get to know us. Isn't that why you been following me around today?" chided Lee Roy.

Jean asked, "Did you pee your pants just a bit, Trooper Princes"

At this point Big John had brought out several of the security personnel and Lee Roy and Jean wanted to get back to safety with backup on the way. "All right, Trooper Princes, we just going to go over here with our big brothers. If you want to chat after your big brothers get here you let us know," said Lee Roy.

Jean said, "We can have us a party, Cajun style, when the rest get here, nice meeting you Trooper Princes." The men walked back to their security team laughing like it had been a good time. Neither of them knew if the trooper had noticed the cameras outside at the top of the building but he should have. The whole thing was on DVR. Trooper Princes cancelled the call for backup but one unmarked car came around the corner to stop at the Trooper's cruiser and who should step out but Special Agent Rogers. Now they had a video record of that as well. Lee Roy turned and yelled out, "Hi there Special Agent Rogers Rabbit! Say hello to Jessica for me!" He smiled big and waved hard in the air. Then he turned and told security, "Wave at the nice Morons!"

Of course, they did and they all had a good laugh about it. Lee Roy slapped Jean on the back and shook Big John's hand, "I got to get home." He got back in his car and sped off before security went back inside and honked and waved as he went past Trooper Princes and Special Agent Rogers Rabbit. Jean would have a copy made of the DVR footage and have it sent over to the attorneys. Lee Roy had brought a whole new level of chess to the game and everyone but the law was enjoying it; enjoying it maybe just a little too much.

Lee Roy got home in plenty of time to see the handywork of the company securing the home for Momma and Angelique. The cameras, motion detectors and new steel doors were all in and the bars over the windows were just being completed with the foot pedal release in case of fire. There were even motion detectors in several places in the yard. Maybe a bit of overkill but after the events of the past few days he was thinking; maybe not so much. The supervisor on the job told Lee Roy the steel bars for the doors wouldn't be ready until tomorrow some time but that he would bring them over personally. Lee Roy was good with that. He felt elated they had gotten so much done on short notice and in only half a day. But the windows and doors were all standard size so the materials could just be picked up from a warehouse.

If the feds came in here, they would have to work at it. The supervisor, Sam, asked if there was any special reason for such extreme measures? Lee Roy loved the look on Sam's face when he said, "Well, you know; black family living in a white neighborhood..." He waited for the look on Sam's face to dawn that he was just pulling his leg and they both got a good laugh. Lee Roy told him the God's honest truth that the feds had been harassing him because of his job at the casino but he didn't go into detail.
"Do you mind if I tell that part to my men?"
"No, but lead with the black family in a white neighborhood part first; they'll get big a kick out of it."
Sam agreed that he would and he walked off smiling. Lee Roy had that effect on folks and it was one of his endearing qualities.

Everything was centralized in the basement office that Lee Roy had never used and Sam took him down stairs with Angelique to show them how to operate everything. They caught on fast as it was all very intuitive and it had now been converted to a safe room as well with its own steel door. It had a rest room already and Sam suggested they stock some dried and canned goods in there just for GP's (General Purposes) along with a small propane stove and electric lanterns in case the power was ever cut. A small metal shelf had been set up to hold batteries a charger and an inverter and Sam gave Lee Roy and Angelique a list of accessories they might want to run down there. Sam would bring four twelve-volt lithium-ion batteries tomorrow if Lee Roy wanted; of course he would…

"We had discussed the price and payment, are you prepared to do that now?"
"I know you said guaranteed funds, like a cashier's check…"
Lee Roy could see Sam's discomfort with what he thought was coming next but Lee Roy couldn't help but laugh and he asked, "Is cash okay?"
Sam was shocked and stammered, "S, Sure, if you've got that kind of cash."
Lee Roy told Sam to turn around and close his eyes while he accessed the safe in the corner of the room.
While he entered the code on the electronic key pad he said to Sam, "You know, I don't run around town, I don't do drugs and I get a sizable check working where I do. So, it's easy to save money."
The next thing Sam heard was a counting machine running hundreds.
"Turn around brother," was Lee Roy's next sentence.
Before he pulled the bills from the machine, he asked Sam to look at the counter. $20,000.00
"There you go my man; I hope that's guaranteed enough for you."
"Thank you, Mr. Pope!"
"No sir, thank you for making it happen so quickly and so well."

Except for the steel bars and the batteries, the job had taken only eight hours from noon until that evening and they were both very happy with the results. Sam and his crew left smiling after they'd cleaned up everything. Lee Roy escorted them out the front door which gave him the opportunity to check up and down the street. "Damn!"

Sam looked at Lee Roy, he pointed at the cruisers, two at either end of the block. Four of them total this time. Sam got a wry smile on his face and said, "Watch this my black brother in a white hood!"

Lee Roy busted a gut and said, "That almost sounded Klan like! All right, impress me."

Sam called his guys around and made a deal with them to pay their tickets if they did as he asked. Lee Roy had never expected it but five rednecks and their boss tore out of there, spinning cookies in the intersections at either end of the block and tearing down the road like raped apes with their hair on fire! Every house in the block opened their front doors and watched the smoke show from tires burning. And the patrol cars that had no choice but to pull them over.

"Thanks, every one! Lee Roy called out. Hope you enjoyed the show from my red neck brothers! They'll be back all this week to put on another show for you!" He waved away the tire smoke from in front of his face coughing. The neighborhood clapped and cheered for they knew his personality and that there must be a good reason. It was a great end to an even better day. Lee Roy went inside and took momma and Angelique downstairs and they set the alarm from there even though there were key pads at the two doors. Lee Roy wanted them all to witness the screen responses to the commands. He showed momma how the room was a safe room and how they could survive down there for a couple of weeks if needed. They had a phone and a radio and could see everything around the house. There was even a generator if they needed it and it was vented to the roof.

"What have you gotten yourself into, Lee Roy?" was momma's response.

"Not me momma, they just have it in for a black man doing well for himself and his family, as far as I can tell."

"Are your friends Max and Ida aware of what's going on?"

"Yes, momma and they're paying for the attorneys involved as well."

"Well, I sure like what I know of them. I'd like to meet them some day."

"I hope that will happen momma. They like what they know of you."

"All right then, I think it's time for me to go to bed."

"We need to also, momma."

Angelique and Lee Roy kissed their momma good night and she went up to bed. Angelique hugged Lee Roy and thanked him for making them secure. She felt she could sleep better tonight; so did Lee Roy. He had the drink he'd not finished the other night… last night? He didn't even remember at this point and it didn't matter. He laid his head down and was out.

In the morning, they left the security up until it was time for Lee Roy to leave for work. There were no patrol cars this morning and no doubt the feds and the locals knew they wouldn't be walking in the front door at Lee Roy's place. If he could, he would have had fifty caliber chain guns installed at all the windows and doors but having multiple DVRs and a safe room would suffice for now. It was a good morning with his family as he was no longer worried about their safety. It had been expensive but it was worth it for his family. Max was heavy on his mind because if not for him, not only would he not need this security but he might already be lying dead in a gutter by the road he had been on. He much preferred this option. He just couldn't believe this all had seemingly been set off by a black man buying a car for cash. That's what it was and Lee Roy knew it in his heart; a sad statement in today's climate but everyone knew those people existed.

Someone had it in for him because he had been frugal with the outrageous salary he made. Ida had been right about not spending it all in one place, he probably should have gone out of town to buy the cars. Water under the bridge now and everyone was dealing with the aftermath. Max had not brought up what Lee Roy believed was the root cause and that's why Lee Roy had done so. He wanted it all out in the open and he wanted it all to be dealt with succinctly. They all had thought it had been with the first purging of agents but that apparently just upset someone. With the second round, the powers that be had learned there was no end to the ability of Max's people.

Now any possibility to hit Lee Roy at home had been blocked by legal means and whoever it was that wanted him so badly would need to rethink their plan. He was fully expecting them to hit him between home and work but was hoping the work the attorneys were doing would put the kibosh on anything like that. Lee Roy had been watching constitutional amendment auditing videos and it seemed the biggest thing would be to keep his nose clean, record video and not cooperate with an obviously illegal stop. Angelique would be taking her car into the local stereo place to have a police type video system installed today. A mobile truck from the same place would be installing the same system in his vehicle at work today. Lee Roy believed that anymore, that type of precaution was required because those in the legal system were worse than the criminals.

He had made it to work while deep in thought and didn't even realize it. There were no patrol cars and no obvious unmarked cars this morning. Maybe the attorneys had accomplished their goal in bringing charges for Rogers Rabbit clocking Lee Roy. He was sure he'd hear on that eventually. It was just nice not to want security to walk him in the employee door today; it almost felt like things were normal again. He went to his office and waved to Sean on his way by his door. Sean followed him into his office and closed the door.

"The attorneys have a case against Rogers Rabbit; I thought you might like to know. Security footage was conclusive and the extra footage of him talking to the local guy out back will probably cause him to lose his job. But, of course, no guarantees."

"Well, that's something anyway. They had four patrol cars outside my house last night watching the security system being installed. My redneck brothers that installed it tore out of there like bats out of hell and drew them off. It was quite a smoke show!"

"Wish I could have been there to see that! Any problems this morning?"

"Nada. I didn't see a stake out, no tail, nobody waiting here."

"That's good. It's probably not over but they received the message. Okay, I'm out of here. Be good."

"Always, Sean. Always."

Another day, another curiosity by the lack of attention from the feds at this point. Katey Sherwood called and let him know she had her son taken care of and that she'd be into work. Lee Roy knew she would and she didn't really need to call but he thanked her. She was due in in just a few minutes but it seemed she must live close to be able to make it in on time. Many of the serving staff lived close at hand, many within walking distance.

"Hi, Mr. Pope!"

Speak of the devil, "Hi, Katey!"

He felt good for her. She was clearly happy today and he felt it was going to be a good day.

CHAPTER EIGHT: THE REASONS FRIENDSHIPS DIE

Ida loved Lee Roy like a son and Max felt the same way. The years rolled past after Special Agent Rogers Rabbit disappeared from the scene and they had never heard from him again. At times they all wondered what had happened to him but there was never any word. Katey Sherwood had married a man in the military that seemed to be a wonderful father to her son and moved to Arlington, Texas. Sean went to work as the manager of the Jackpot Casino when Max and his friends/partners bought it. That put Lee Roy on the night shift which wasn't his idea of a good time but it was more responsibility and therefore more money. He couldn't very well refuse more money. And things seemed to be going very well for everyone.

As Ida thought back to those times, she was saddened they had not continued and as she told the story to Charles and Jim, she teared up a couple of times. It was obviously very emotional for her; she'd had a very deep love for Max, Lee Roy and everyone in their lives back then. It seemed to Charles and Jim that something catastrophic had to have happened to destroy the empire and drive such a deep wedge between The Three Musketeers as Max, Ida and Lee Roy had begun to call themselves way back when. Max had bought the house in Dallas about that time so that he could retire away from the front office, the underground and the casinos. He had enjoyed all of it at the time and although he wanted to keep his finger on the pulse, he felt there was no reason to stay in Shreveport where he felt they were too close for comfort with the ever-increasing pressure from other organizations, the Feds again and recent incursions by the local po-po. Besides that, his family had always had close ties to Dallas in one way or another and he was comfortable there.

The fragile egg of their world cracked one evening without warning when Momma and Angelique had disappeared from the super grocery parking lot. Their car had been found abandoned with all the doors and trunk open. Groceries gone for the most part from thieves and nothing on the vehicle DVR; mostly because it had been ripped out. Of course, no one had seen a thing and even the super grocery cameras had not caught anything as they'd been turned off for that moment. Someone with pull had accomplished the kidnapping. Lee Roy was devastated and beside himself with angst. He almost went completely around the bend when mommas body was found in pieces on the railroad tracks two days later. It was so mangled they almost had not found the bullet hole in the eye socket that had been the real cause of death. At least she had died quickly. Lee Roy had been called to the coroner's office to identify what was left of her. And it was not good on him; he could only identify her hair line and the dress she was wearing, the wedding ring she still wore on her ring finger. But they knew it wasn't a robbery for the wedding ring to be left behind. It was left on purpose to identify her.

He'd gone home and locked himself away without a word to anyone. The other managers at The Golden Oyster covered for him without question. From what they could tell after the fact, Lee Roy had received a note taped to one of his outside cameras thus blocking the view. He noticed it and he had retrieved it. It had lain on his desk until the police finally found it during the ensuing investigation after Max's death. It had been type written and had no discernable artifacts to identify where it had originated. It just told Lee Roy to show up at the train yard at three a.m. of a night specified if he wanted his sister to live. When he got there, he found out what had happened to Special Agent Rogers Rabbit. The psychopath couldn't help but tell him how he'd lost his job, his house and his wife because of Lee Roy and Max's lawyers. No one would hire him anywhere in the entire US because of what had happened and the department having to pay out millions to Oyster and to Lee Roy.

Rogers Rabbit told Lee Roy that he was to betray Max in such a way that the entire empire would fall. Lee Roy had a choice but it meant betraying his beloved friend Max or his sister's death. Lee Roy refused. The next day, Angelique's ring finger arrived in a small box left on Lee Roy's front porch. He got a call from a burner phone and the voice on the other end was unmistakably that of Rogers Rabbit, "One more time, you do as you're told or your sister dies. This is your last chance." The line went dead. Lee Roy knew that the deranged man meant what he said after what had been done to his mother. He didn't even dare go to Max with this, he didn't feel he had a choice. He knew his sister would die if he tried to fix the situation and he saw no way out. He went to the FBI to report Rogers Rabbit but they refused to do anything unless he gave them whatever information it was that Rogers wanted him to reveal. And so, he had. He gave them everything he knew of the underground. That's all he had; he didn't even have information on the wood chipper. He had never seen it and no one had told him anything more. They arrested Lee Roy under the RICO (Racketeer Influenced and Corrupt Organizations) act but gave him a deal for six months in exchange for his house. A raid was planned on the underground from the information he had provided.

Max died in the supposed cross fire but everyone knew better. Ida was devastated, Lee Roy couldn't believe how they had killed so many in a firefight that never happened, Max had not allowed weapons in the underground. That didn't mean they weren't there, everyone knew they had weapons, but it was not the firefight the FBI claimed and there were no deaths of Agents while almost everyone in the underground was at the very least, seriously injured. It was like shooting fish in a barrel. The final report claimed that all the deaths were justified shootings but everyone knew it was retribution for the wood chipper incident. Ida had gotten off Scot-free because she knew nothing and was still just a front office secretary. No one would testify against her anyway, not even Lee Roy. There was no evidence they found that could connect her to the underground, she only registered debits and credits for the front office. Now she lived in Dallas anyway and had not actually been officially employed for several months. The house was solely hers as the co-owner and with Max dead the feds could make no claim on it. They certainly tried but her attorneys made short work of that.

The Jackpot Casino and The Golden Oyster could not be implicated although they had both been shut down for a while during the investigation. The attorneys got them both open again as there were investors with money involved in addition to Max. It didn't take long before the underground was demolished and filled with concrete. While this was going on, Lee Roy tried to contact Rogers and the feds claimed they had out a nationwide search going on but to no avail. Rogers had disappeared and Angelique was never heard from again. Lee Roy arranged for a storage for his vehicles and the boxes of cash he had stashed before the feds took his house.

No one knew of the money and his redneck friend in security, Sam, had helped him obtain a small property where they'd built Lee Roy a garage with a built in safe; all of it underground. Lee Roy had paid Sam double the value for the storage and it was built to something of a military standard. It was not likely Sam would risk the relationship as he knew his discretion would get him more work with Lee Roy. What Lee Roy had already paid him had been invested wisely and Sam's business had prospered dramatically. Sam was completely above board but he had no issue working with a criminal as generous as Lee Roy. Besides, Lee Roy seemed to be more of a criminal by happenstance than by nature. Sam could live with that.

Everything was complete when Lee Roy went to prison to serve his time. He ended up serving an extra six months for assault on another prisoner that had made the mistake of thinking Lee Roy was just another snot nosed rich kid. There was nothing but respect for Lee Roy inside after that. The other guy was transferred to another facility as he wasn't quite right in the head anymore and it was deemed unsafe for him to be among the regular population. Lee Roy was only convicted because they could, not because he was guilty as he took three massive blows form the other guy before he half killed him. Lee Roy was almost out of prison before the other guy was considered recovered; he wasn't really recovered, only physically. Had the prison psychologist been honest he would have listed Joshua Grant as criminally insane. Lee Roy had broken something in the man's head and he'd meant to do it. Franky had taught him things that others would not have.

Lee Roy left prison on a rainy Sunday morning, in Louisiana it was Eighty degrees Fahrenheit and ninety percent humidity when the rain wasn't coming down. He'd barely stepped outside when he broke a drenching sweat that had his crotch wringing wet before he made his way around to the front of the prison. He walked into the lobby and used the bank card he'd hidden under the insole of his tennis shoe and retrieved the hundred dollar bills he'd left under there as well. The desk officer behind the glass called her shift supervisor when she saw what he had hidden there but there was no longer anything they could do about it. He wasn't inside and it couldn't be considered contraband anymore. He used the bank card to call a cab and made a show of putting the hundred-dollar bills into his wallet that they'd cleaned out. The system was set up to remove any ability for the released convict to be able to have cash on hand when they got out, a little parting gift. They were given a check to compensate for any cash they may have had going in but it was often drawn on an out of state bank. The entire system was intended to punish even after the sentence was served.

His cab arrived and he gave instructions to take him to his property and vehicles. It was a two-hundred-dollar cab ride but Lee Roy had the key and combination to get in through the man door done in under a minute once he got there. He fired up the generator, turned on some lights, keyed in the code on the safe, replaced the internal batteries just for GPs and put twenty thousand in his shoes and wallet. He pulled the cover from his Avalon and started it up to get the Aircon running before he pulled it out. The generator ran a one-horse motor on a hydraulic pump to lift the one-inch-thick steel garage door. He pulled his baby out started bumping the stereo while he closed down his private storage. He had nothing left in Shreveport so he was heading for Dallas to start a new life. This time, he would be in charge. The entire time he'd been inside he thought of Max and Ida and he couldn't imagine what she'd thought of him this entire time. He only wished he could take back the decisions he'd made in the end. He was only trying to save his siter but Ida would never forgive him after it cost her everything.

He'd been to Deep Ellum a couple of times and he knew that was the place to make the necessary contacts to start new. The money he had on hand would get him a stake in the local drug game without any problem, all he needed to do was avoid any deep cover cops. Easier said than done but he was going to take that chance. Most people thought that flashing cash was the way to get into the local trade but that was just a good way to get rolled. When he got to town, he found a court and started playing some B-ball with the local brothers. He rented a room in a local dive hotel to flop and bought some clothes to fit the scene. He had clothes back at the storage but he knew those were too nice and wouldn't fly with what he was doing. He went to eat at the local chicken and ribs joint where he saw some of the brothers from the court. He assumed they had money to eat out so they might know what he needed to know. He pulled in with them and talked about his momma and sister and how they died; how he was starting over in Dallas to get away from the memories.

Within a week he had a number for the local supplier and one of the brothers from the court, Vinny, was going to go with him to vouch for him. He set up the meeting naming his friend and he would be in with a bigger name in town. This was just a meet and greet and he knew it was the most dangerous part of setting up a connection. Everyone would be on edge. He and Vinny went in to introduce him to man known only as Kong. There was a reason for that, too. He had to be seven feet tall and Lee Roy was only five foot ten inches. The muscle in the room was all over six foot and Lee Roy felt like a Lilly-Putian in the land of the giants. Kong seemed like a reasonable guy but he wanted numbers, how much did Lee Roy expect to move? Lee Roy said that with Kong's help he could move as much as he could supply. Kong wasn't buying it and said he smelled like a narc. One of the muscles moved in and Lee Roy went into action, an elbow to the solar plexus and heal on his arch a throat punch and then grabbed him by the head and flipped him to the ground. The others moved in; Lee Roy shouted, "you know about Max in Shreveport?" That got some attention. "He trained me."

Kong responded, "You mean Franky trained you."

"Well, that too. But Max was my friend"

"Okay, I'm listening."

"I've got ten large today and I can pay cash tomorrow for as much as you want to move. I just need your help setting up a network that won't get me hung. I'm new in town and I need to get my cash flow going without catching a case."

"This is my side of town," said Kong, "You'll have to go to the other side so you don't step on my toes."

"Done," said Lee Roy.

"Come into my inner sanctum," said Kong, "Get Jefferson cleaned up," he told the others. "Jefferson shouldn't have moved on you like that. Vinny, you coming too?"

"Yes."

Kong nodded.

Kong poured some cheap whisky in his little bedroom office. And they toasted to Jefferson's recovery.

"I met Franky and Max years ago, too bad what happened to them."

"Ya, too bad," said Lee Roy. "It still hurts me."

"You were pretty close?"

"Close enough for first names at dinner."

"That's close. I heard someone ratted him out."

"I don't know for sure; I was working at The Golden oyster when it went down. I ended up doing a short case for RICO."

"Sorry to know that. Max was a legend. Okay, I'm going to get you set up if you're serious about doing all I can give you."

"I've got whatever you need for cash as long as you don't up charge more than your share."

"Vinny here will tell you, I'm good to my peeps."

"I don't know either of you that well but once upon a time, Max took a pistol right out of my hand, he took a chance on a punk kid and he changed my entire life. I'm hoping we can help each other like that."

"That's what I'm talking about," responded Kong.

They spent the next hour talking details and Lee Roy even told Kong about his private storage, not where it was but what it was. He told Kong about the front office and how he thought he could pull that off here in Dallas, maybe even the underground. Kong was salivating like one of Pavlov's dogs at what Lee Roy was suggesting. The numbers Kong was suggesting told Lee Roy that his cash was not endless but it was comparable to what Lee Roy had; that was significant.

* * *

Ida had done a great deal of research on Lee Roy to learn all of this and she was bound and determined to see him go down for what he'd done to Max and his operation. Her pain was obvious and it was a poisonous crucifixion that she planned to bring against Lee Roy. She knew he was operating out of a warehouse between Dallas and Fort Worth With a small, separate front office similar to what Max had established. No one could tell it had anything to do with the warehouse and the landfill being done on the property proved that he was building his own underground starting with a passage from the front office to the nearby warehouse. It had taken Max and his predecessors three generations to establish their business but Lee Roy had the advantage of an abundance of cash, a well-to-do partner and a ready-made market on two sides. He had established a small strip mall next to his front office and then he had opened a hip hop club in the strip mall with a delivery pizza restaurant to validate the traffic in and out at all hours of the day and night. It was the perfect set up to have his runners coming in and out all day and all night with no one the wiser. The warehouse was reputedly used for all the stores in the strip mall to excuse the heavy truck traffic and no one seemed to question the use of such a facility.

Because of the highways they traveled, the runners had crotch rockets instead of scooters. There were many tales in the employee break room in the warehouse of out running the cops at night. They didn't run that many trips during the day because of the traffic, that's when the trucks would run, but at night they'd bring in and send out small shipments all the way from El Paso, Santa Fe and Albuquerque on occasion. Lee Roy and Kong had gotten their system set up and operational with Vinny's help in only two years and they had even been honored in both the Dallas and the Fort Worth Chambers of Commerce. Ida suspected there had been some payoffs involved. To anyone looking on, it appeared to be a legit operation and that was the rub. Ida, Charles and Jim had to come up with a con that would enrich themselves and destroy Lee Roy, Kong and Vinny. They had an idea and they were going to feel the current before long to see if it could fly. Jim was a great I.T. guy and Charles was no slouch either. They had found several chinks in the armor for the business and they had put together some ideas that now needed sewing up.

With Lee Roy busy building his underground and the long-distance network for running drugs, he'd completely forgotten about locating Benny, in fact, Benny wondered who the gang bangers in the blue Chevelle had been since Lee Roy was operating almost on the opposite side of the metroplex. Jim retrieved much his belongings and a great deal of his cash money and brought them into Ida's place in Dallas. Along with those he brought a great deal of computer equipment although most of it was in the way of applications on his laptop. He also had storage and I.P. equipment making him look like an address that shifted around the world.

The nearly doubled drug problem in the metroplex was being blamed on the traffic coming across the open Southern border and Lee Roy was taking full advantage of the media confusion to build the distribution for he, Kong and Vinny. That was the beauty of the underground, it kept out prying eyes and gave the appearance there was no central hub when in fact that was the backbone of the operation. Even some of his networks were building smaller versions around the area in order to take on larger shipments and that added another level of confusion for the DEA and FBI. They simply couldn't identify the legs of this spider and the body was completely invisible.

That's where I.T. was going to come into play. Lee Roy was using it to set up his network and although he was wise in using encryption and hiding his I.P. address, Jim found all the information and had it on a thumb drive. Unfortunately, Lee Roy and probably Kong and Vinny knew of both Jim and Ida but they didn't know Charles. Charles, not the most competent but still quite good at I.T. would have to be the front man of the operation and he was going to breach boldly the front store in a manner to blow the minds of all three partners. He was going to walk right in and tell them all about themselves. Ida didn't know if Lee Roy had employed the use of a wood chipper at this point as that seemed unique to Max's operations but if he had, Charles would be risking finding out. The plan was going to be a matter of exposing the weakness of their internet and appear to bolster it while setting up a direct route to the FBI with a single switch to turn it on at the right time.

It was brilliant in its simplicity and hinged only on Charle's initial performance. Either he convinced them or he would likely die and the odds were running to him succeeding due to all the deep information Ida and Jim had been able to put together. That's where the leverage to ask for a percentage of the operation would come in. That's where the con would be seated. Upon flipping the switch to expose the operation, the new and improved version of The Three Musketeers would take what truly belonged to Ida. Not just a percentage but every stinking copper penny from every account, all cash accounts and even a good deal of what they had in bundles of ten thousands. That was the stickiest part but it would likely work and be by their own hands.

The day came that Charles had to walk in and risk his life for the team. Following Ida's advice, he was bold and parked directly in front of the front office. He sat there for a few moments until he was certain he'd been seen and had garnered enough attention to be considered a possible problem. Most sales people walked right in because sales were based on numbers and time was of the essence. Unless they could set a hook they wanted to be after the next fish. Charles made it perfectly clear that he had all the time in the world and when he exited the vehicle, he was slow and methodical making any one watching painfully aware that he didn't care what they were thinking. He carried only two things, a thin manila folder with a few papers in it and a thumb drive with the entire kingdom on it. He walked in the front door in total confidence to be greeted by the cute young receptionist, and all three of the partners. The men stood at the back and let Janette address this stranger.

"Hello, sir, how may I help you today?"
"I'm here to see the owners of the company."
"The partners aren't in today; I can leave them a message if you'd like."
"Your name is Janette, is that correct?"
Janette was obviously surprised that Charles knew her name. Nobody should know her name. "Yes, that's correct."
"I know you are just doing your job and you pulled off a believable performance. But that is the first and the last time you should ever try to lie to me."
Janette turned to look at the partners as that's exactly where Charles was looking. He had not even looked Janette in the eye

when he told her she'd lied to him.

Charles stepped up to Lee Roy first as he knew Lee Roy was in charge. He offered his hand and said, "Lee Roy, I'm Charles."

He turned next to Kong and shook his hand saying, "Kong, I'm happy to make your acquaintance and I hope you never get angry and sit on me." Kong's mouth dropped open at the boldness of the humor and the fact that Charles knew his name. Last, he turned to Vinny and offered his hand and greeted him. Now he controlled the room and they would either kill him or give him an audience. The latter was more likely as he'd shown superior knowledge and preparation for the meeting.

"I'd like to save your lives and a likely Twenty-five to life in prison sentence for each and every one of you. Your operation, as careful as you are, is exposed and we should talk privately. Sorry, Janette, I probably shouldn't have said that in front of you but you're going to be getting a pretty good size raise tomorrow. So, just forget this ever happened."

Janette looked the partners in the face, her own face turning red and turned around to mind her own business.

"I hope you don't mind gentlemen; can we retire to the main room here where we can get comfortable for about a half an hour? I'm sorry to take you by surprise like that but I needed to impress you with the importance of what I want to discuss with you."

"You got our attention, Mr., now convince us why we shouldn't delete you from the face of the earth," said Vinny.

"Fair enough, Vinny. I'd probably feel the same way if some yahoo walked in from the street claiming to know everything about me. Let's start with your employee list and how much you pay each one of them."

Charles put the manila folder on the table between them and flipped open the cover. There were the names and the salaries of every one of the runners, warehouse people, truck drivers and Janette. Janette's name was circled and her salary showed written over by a number that was double what she made now.

"She knows a lot more than you think she does and as she seems to be loyal and very sweet, I suspect you want to keep her around. You should start paying her that figure I've shown by tomorrow or you'll have to find someone new in just a few weeks."

Lee Roy looked at the other two and said, "He's probably right." Kong and Vinny nodded their heads. "Okay, keep talking."

"You've got a laptop in here, haven't you?"

Vinny stood and pulled one out of the top drawer of the wooden filing cabinet. He plugged it in and let it boot up.

"Have you got Exell on there?"

"Yes," responded Vinny.

"I actually knew that already."

Charles pulled the thumb drive from his breast pocket and handed it to Vinny.

"There's only one Exell file on there and lots of photos. Open the Exell file for now, we can look at the photos later."

Vinny did as requested, and all three men visibly shrank from the plethora of information the file contained.

"That's why Max used to keep everything on a hand written ledger," said Charles. "If I could pull that from your computers, eventually, the FBI and the DEA will find the way in the back door that I found. That's not to say it was easy, it took me a couple of months to weasel my way in; I had a goal and I wanted it badly enough to figure it out. But you are completely exposed. I can fix the whole thing. For a price."

"What's your price?" asked Kong.

"I'm not greedy, I was thinking ten percent of net profits while I work for you. That would be less than half of what each of you make. I wouldn't even ask for a partnership; I just want to be paid a reasonable price for my services and when I'm done, I'll be out of your hair forever and you'll never hear from me again."

The three men looked at each other and Kong spoke, "I imagine there are dire consequences if we refuse?"

"You would imagine right. But my price is fair and I would leave you with an uncrackable system. I go away after it's completed and we all live happy lives."

Charles was obviously strong arming them but he was making a reasonable offer for compensation and he certainly had the goods on them. Kong continued, "We need a day to talk it over. I don't see how we can refuse but I want to discuss it with Lee Roy and Vinny."

Charles seemed genuinely sincere when he said, "I would expect nothin less considering how I brought this to you. Keep the thumb drive to look at it at your leisure."

The partners just dismissed him with a backhanded wave as if to shew him away and they stared at the screen of the laptop. He left a cryptic business card on the table with nothing but a local phone number and a photo of their own front office; the initial C. at the bottom. Charles left the office, got back in the Caprice and started shaking from the adrenalin rush the whole thing had been. He had pulled off some pretty great performances in the past but this was certainly one of the top five. This one was fraught with real danger from real criminals.

"How did I do," he said to no one.

The bug in his ear answered back, "You get an academy award for that performance. Congratulations, you have them by the short hairs," said Jim.

"I'll see you soon and we can have a celebratory drink."

"Roger," came back both Ida and Jim.

It took the entire drive back to Ida's for Charles to calm down. The entire way he made a convoluted trip back home just in case someone was following him. He didn't notice anyone. He parked to the side of the drive and covered the car, more to ensure no one could find it if they happened to be looking, than for Ida's embarrassment. He was just glad the initial meet and greet was over as that was the most dangerous moment. He knew they would be trying to find out who he was but he was more of a ghost than any of the rest of them. It was time to dump the Caprice and get something else for the next thirty days.

There were some Note lots over in Garland; lots that caried the note on used cars for folks that couldn't get a loan for a lack of credit. Those vehicles would be well checked mechanically because if they stopped running, the new owners would quit paying for them and leave them where they died. Charles spotted out an AMC Eagle Talon on one of the lots and had Ida drop him nearby so that he could walk in. The Eagle

Talon was an across-the-board racing machine and there were versions sold under Mitsubishi, Dodge, Plymouth and Chrysler. This had the TSi indication on the fender which could mean it was an actual Turbo Sport Intercooled model. It could also mean someone just bought the designation and placed it on the fender to try and look cool. The thing Charles had to watch for on this vehicle was to be sure the turbo, if it actually had one, had not been coked up. That's where the turbocharger is not allowed to cool sufficiently before stopping the motor. The oil in the bearings fries and seizes the turbo. These vehicles were too old to have a listed resale value so he would just have to dicker with the sales person on the lot.

The man fair ran out the door of the office and introduced himself as Reverend Jones and Charles about laughed in his face. At least he knew he was a con man dealing with a con man. He decided to try and throw the man off his game and just be straight up with him.

"Okay, Reverend, I want this Talon. If the price is right, I've got cash."

"You've got cash?"

"That's right, give me your best price for me to drive it off the lot before two p.m. Why don't you pop the hood and let me take a look at the turbo."

"You know something about these cars?"

"I know if the turbo is coked it's not worth more than the tow truck to haul it away."

Reverend Jones stopped dead and exclaimed, "I sell nothing but quality, A#1 vehicles to my customers!"

"I'm sure that's true Reverend. Pop the hood for me, please."

The Reverend seemed truly offended but he might just be a great actor as well. He opened the door and reached inside for the hood lever. Charles raised the hood and there sat a brand-new turbo and intercooler. It had likely had been run hard but it had been properly cared for by someone. There wasn't even any dirt on the underside of the spark plugs. The detail job was immaculate. The waste gate was aftermarket which might be why the intercooler had been replaced. Too much boost from an over pressure waste gate would split an intercooler.

The intercooler was stock so that could be exactly what had happened.

"What's your price, Reverend?"
"Don't you want to drive it?"
"Of course, but I want to know what I'm looking at before I waste my time."
"$5000.00 even."
The reverend watched for a reaction but Charles gave nothing up.
"Let me take it for a test drive and if it checks out, I'll give you $4500.00, no questions asked."
"You're a man that knows the value of this vehicle. If I let you test drive it, you'll be happy to pay the $5000.00."
Charles laughed, the reverend was right, "Okay, let's give you my I.D.; I want to drive it first but I'll pay your price."
That put a smile on Reverend Jone's face. He knew they understood each other all too well. Jones could get $5000.00 for that car all day long and Charles was lucky it wasn't already sold. They stepped into the small office and the reverend took Charles fake I.D. and copied it. He handed over the key to the Talon and sat back knowing he had this sale in the bag. The good reverend, a con man himself also knew that Charles knew his stuff and would be impressed with how the vehicle drove out. So it was that Charles came back from the test drive and shelled out $5000.00 for the car and was happy to do it. There was no smoke when he started it, he could hear the turbo operating as he ran it up onto IH-635 that ran nearby and it shifted through all five manual gears like clockwork. The AC was cold and everything seemed to work the way it was intended. Charles pulled the money from his pocket and they counted it together.

This little car was quicker than most cars and could keep up with some of the crotch rockets of the day. It had plenty of room in the front for two people and the seats in back although tiny would accommodate Benny with no problem. One reason Charles wanted it was because of the possibility of a street chase with the thugs with which he was becoming involved. Any advantage for his safety was to be considered. The zero to sixty time advertised was six point three seconds which was quite respectable. Charles didn't anticipate any issues but it was better to be prepared and not need, than to need and not be prepared. He drove back to Ida's knowing this car would be much more acceptable to her because of its reputation as a street monster. It seemed odd to him that it had never become the classic performance vehicle for which it had built such a solid reputation, but it was a cult classic and he enjoyed the low-key popularity of it.

On the drive back to Ida's he got a call from Lee Roy who simply said they had considered his proposal and wanted to hear more. They wanted him to come over right away. He called Ida and let her and Jim know but they insisted he come and get his wires so they could listen also. The latest equipment was so easily hidden because what they had, used the front office internet connection. After all they had the password so why not take advantage of it. That way Jim and Ida didn't have to be nearby to listen in or give their two bits to his spiel. He made a quick stop home as it was almost directly on the way and put the bug in his ear and the microphone glued to his scalp under his hair. It was flesh-tone so no one would notice unless they knew what to look for.

Benny made a big deal over the car because he was a bit of a car buff himself and he knew the vehicle inside and out for what it was capable. Not too many years more and it would be considered a classic. But it was in far better shape than most cars that age. Kids these days might never know the incredible cars they had missed out on over the years. Not that today's cars had not come back to a point of respectability but after the anemic cars of the seventies and eighties this car was a true breath of fresh air that could still hold its own. Ida couldn't figure out what all the fuss was about.

The day was quickly getting away from them before Charles got out the door to meet at the front office again. When he pulled up, they walked out to greet him and the first thing they noticed was his new car.
Kong said, "Spending your money already, I see."

"I take it you mean to hire me?"

"You don't leave us with much choice. Your terms are acceptable and this is your first day on the job. Impress us."

Charles shot back, "You're already impressed or I wouldn't be here, alive and happy to help out."

The partners laughed because they knew he was absolutely right in all respects.

"All right, let's go inside, it's too hot out here for human life."

Inside the main room Charles made himself at home laying out a pre-typed set of instructions for setting up a virtual private network on their router. He explained this as he set up their laptop, he told them he would use only their equipment so that he couldn't key log his strokes and walk away with any more information than he'd already shown them. Which was plenty; this made the three very happy. The latest technology used a data base of internet service provider (ISP) addresses that it would rotate through on an hourly basis. It only required that Charles set up a small executable program that ran in the background and clocked off of the international time clock that was a part of every ISP information packet. Charles explained that if they had other routers, he would need to do the same thing with those. If he set up each one with a random rotating data base it would create a web of lies no one could track. At this location alone there would be three routers he could set in this manner. The front office, the warehouse and the Hip Hop bar at the other end of the complex. All of the rest of the businesses were hard wired into one of the two in the strip mall and he was working on one of them. He recommended they set up some of their larger distributors with the same program. That would mean setting up an appointment for Charles to visit them and use their own equipment to set up the same information and rotating data base.

This would only hide their locations and he wanted to set up end to end encryption between the front office and all of their locations next. He also set up a password of their choosing on each Router, he suggested they use something different for each router. The whole time Jim Benny was taking notes over the hidden microphone that transmitted over their own internet connection. By the time he was done with the routers at this location he'd spent three hours and it was already the rush hour. Everyone wanted to go home as no one was a slave to their job in this organization and they all agreed to begin at nine a.m. tomorrow. The partners seemed suitably impressed with what Charles did today, especially as he kept them informed with each step he took. Really, that was so Benny could listen and correct him if he made a mistake. Charles was good but not Jim Benny good. He even managed to install the same back door log-in on each router without anyone being the wiser. The partners seemed to be accepting Charles as one of their own and that would make his deception that much easier.

Charles didn't like doing this to the partners as they seemed like top shelf guys that hated the government take just as much as he and Benny. But after what Lee Roy had done to Max and Ida, no matter the reason, they were going down. He had to separate himself from how he felt personally and remember that Lee Roy had stolen the lives of a lot of good people. Regardless of their source of income he'd destroyed a generational business in addition to ending the life of his mentor by proxy. He was fair game and so was anyone running with him.

Jim had written the encryption program but that would require the partners install a server instead of using laptops. It didn't have to be more than a desktop computer with server capabilities. That was barely more than one could buy off the shelf at any computer store. Everything at their end would run through the server to be encrypted and then be sent out over the virtual network. These guys weren't big enough to have a lot of communication but whatever they did have would, by this means, be stored on the server for later exposure. It would be glorious! The only things that wouldn't be stored on the server would be their banking information. They had plenty of that in off shore accounts and all of that information was being sent to Benny real-time. When the time came, Benny would have the information but no one else would not even Lee Roy and his partners unless they had it written down somewhere. The cash would be the only hitch. They had to face facts, cash was cash and it was hard to confiscate it if one didn't know where it was and how to access it. But they were going to try.

Charles was trying to talk these guys into letting him install servers at their larger satellite distribution centers. As well. Once he set them up on random ISP's it would make everything invisible to anyone looking on and the encryption algorithms would make them feel secure enough to talk about anything on line. It only took a week to get the front office set up and secure and Charles was working hard to get their other locations around town, Louisiana Albuquerque to accept the idea of following suit. Of course, the partners had the final say and the other locations, like it or not, would follow suit. The decision was made and Charles would travel to the other locations as required and get them set up as well. It wasn't long before the entire operation was networked in and running through the server in the front office. It took just over five weeks to finish the job and true to his word, Charles would bow out. That was the hitch, the partners wanted to keep him around in case of some type of problem or betrayal. That had not been part of the plan or part of the agreement.

Charles was feeling very bad about this new development, he reminded them that he was still charging them at the agreed upon rate which didn't seem to faze them. He didn't really want to stick around doing nothing with the system up and working flawlessly so he put on his salesman's cap and suggested they let him build a backup unit specifically to download information from the server on a weekly basis. Just in case something happened to their server and it would provide another degree of separation from anyone accessing the information. He told them that although he felt he had fulfilled his end of the bargain that they would have no need of him after he'd done that. It seemed to make them feel warm and fuzzy and the new agreement was struck. The parts were purchased by the next day inclusive to several eight terabyte hard drives; more than they should ever need and Charles went to work with Benny in his ear. This was something Charles had never done so he needed Benny's help. As it turned out it was probably a great idea because now everything could be removed from the server and backed up leaving it less vulnerable to outside access. Except of course for Benny. A single cable between the server and the backup allowed for the backup to occur. What the partners couldn't know was that the very same cable would transfer data back through the server to the internet... while the partners were feeling warm and fuzzy they were as wide open as a window on a hot summer day.

A week later, Charles showed them what and how to do the backup and clear off the server records and he was done. To all appearances everything was secure like a three-tumbler combination lock while Jim Benny had a key to the door on the back of the safe. They paid him and he left a happy man $75,000.00 dollars and change richer. They paid in cash leaving no paper trail as was best for everyone concerned. Charles had not put his Talon through its paces yet but that evening it was time to make the car boogie on down the road. First, he drove toward Fort Worth on IH-30, then down IH-35W south to IH-20, across to the surface streets that took him to the Dallas North Tollway where he drove North and finally back South on the surface streets to Ida's place. It was nice to have Ida and Benny in his ear as he did this, he was feeling like his life was on the line at this point. A matter of having no loose ends but it seemed they weren't going to chase him down. Now it was time to let them use their new system and build information.

When the breach occurred, they wanted it to be so large and convicting that there would never be an operation like this one ever again. And Ida wanted the money to be so huge that no one would believe it. The partners had that kind of loot already but the daily profits were unbelievably large. A data base had to be established showing where the profits were being made and where, off shore, they were being stashed. That would be the crux of the bust; to show where the money was stashed, having a record for the authorities and then hiding from the authorities where it would be transferred. As the weeks passed by to gather the required evidence, Jim was scouring the information they were storing for any indication of the stash points for their cash.

To the credit of the receptionist, Janette, she was keeping immaculate tax records for the front office to make it look like a legitimate business but that gave Benny a clue as to where Lee Roy was stashing his cash. Every other week Benny discovered an entry for gas and food for a business meeting in Louisiana. The consistency of the gas consumption suggested it was always to the same location. To find that location, they would need to somehow place a tracker on Lee Roy's car. The tracking units were easy enough to come by and they could be observed over Google GPS information systems. If people only understood how much information Google assimilated on them there would be an outcry the likes of which had not been heard since the Boston tea party. Everyone learns in school that the Boston tea party was the start of the revolutionary war but that's an outright lie. The British had tried to confiscate guns from the settlers in the new world because of the revolt against taxation and hundreds had died resisting that confiscation.

That's one reason that Charles didn't mind milking fools for their money, they allowed the government tax man to steal from their families' mouths on a daily basis without ever anything more than an ineffective complaint to their neighbor. The banks were even worse driving housing prices ever higher, using fractional banking, trapping people in a death pledge; the foundational meaning of the word mortgage. Mortgage comes from the old French and before that, Latin. Mort being the word for death. A house mortgage is a death trap. If one only looks at how much they have paid in interest and principal alone they have generally paid the bank the full amount of the thirty-year loan in the first ten years. Not only that, but once that money is guaranteed by the debtor, the bank can count that as profit and loan out ten times that amount in new loans; fractional banking. The whole system was all a big scam, a house of cards and joe-blow-honest-working-man was under the load of paying it to everyone but him/herself. It was legalized theft. The so-called good life in the United States was nothing but one big money laundering scam and Charles had no problem finding any way he could to scam that money for himself. Taking it from other criminals was not going to cause him to lose any sleep; especially when those criminals would be doing hard time.

Charles researched the available GPS tracking devices and found one that would work by just sticking it under the plastic bumper cover and the battery was reputed to last for a year. Pretty slick for under a hundred dollars. He knew of a homeless guy that hung out near the front office to rummage through the garbage and beg off the Hip Hop club patrons. He knew Bill to say hello and sometimes gave him some cash. He approached him one evening after the front office had closed and there was relative safety from identification after dark. Charles made it worth his while to take care of placing the device for him the next day when Lee Roy's car was there and promised a pint and small bonus when he confirmed it was working. It was almost too easy; technology had made it such that they would know everything about these guys before long. No wonder Max had been one to do books by hand in all respects of his business.

Within three months Jim had four confirmed hits on a GPS location in Louisiana and Charles and Ida took a drive out to the location. To all appearances it was just a piece of property with no identifying features but for a gravel drive. No mailbox, no address, nothing but open space. They decided to drive down the gravel road and see what there was to see. As they got around four-hundred feet back the road turned hard to the left into a natural outcropping of scrub bushes. Then it descended below ground level to a drainage grate and a solid steel door about the size of a garage with a keypad beside it. They could only assume the key pad was the way into the underground structure so Charles walked down the decline and photographed the key pad and messaged it for Benny's perusal.

They had done all they could for the time being and decided to head back to Dallas. It was a beautiful day and they couldn't help but enjoy the scenery, they stopped in at the Bucky's gas stop South East of Mesquite along the way as those were always a fun spot to people watch and have a quick bight of horrible heart stopping greasy food. Walking back out to the Talon, Charles got a call from Benny. He was excited like a puppy ready to pee himself as he almost yelled over the phone, "Lee Roy is on his way!"

"No! it's not his regular timing!"

"I'm telling you, he's on his way now! He's stopped for the moment but he's on the interstate and he's going to be introducing himself to you if you're not careful."

Charles and Ida got into the Talon and sat there for a moment scanning the parking lot just in case. Bucky's was a popular place to stop but they couldn't imagine actually running into those thugs here. Hopefully that would not be the case. What were the chances?

They left the gas stop and headed up the interstate and didn't see Lee Roy, hopefully he didn't see them either, but who could say? If Charles had run into Lee Roy by himself that would be one thing, just a chance occurrence, but to be with Ida? That would be a very convicting death sentence for them both. They might never live to tell about it. They were back on the highway when Benny called again to let them know that Lee Roy had continued on his way to Shreveport. Everyone breathed a sigh of relief. They had purposely planned this expedition on a weekday as Lee Roy had never made the trip on anything other than a weekend in the past. It gave them pause to wonder why.

Ida had been busy herself these past few months trying to collect on her insurance claim. The company was highly dubious of the theft of such a cash amount in spite of the fact that everything checked out. In fact, it could hardly have been a more perfect theft except that the boys walked away with nothing but a hand written note. Ida still laughed at them over that. She said she only wished she could have seen Jim's face as he read the note; that would have been a hoot! The same insurance inspector had been by several times because he'd 'forgotten' to check one thing or another; just an excuse to come back in the house to see if the money had been spent on something he might spot on the premises.

He certainly made note of the Talon but Charles bragged about the $5000.00 price tag like it was some kind of trophy. In fact, Mr. Johnson happened to be a bit of an aficionado on turbo charged vehicles and they had a great conversation one day about turbo pressures, timing and available reprogramming chips for the microprocessors in turbocharged vehicles. It may or may not have helped convince Mr. Johnson of the validity of the purchase, not that Charles would ever spend much more than that on a vehicle. In his line of work, it paid to be able to dump a car and blow town in a heartbeat. Charles was not above riding a Grey Hound bus to his next destination.

Ida finally had to retain an attorney on the matter of the theft and now it would cost the insurance even more money than had they paid out the principal amount to start with. After all, they had approved the antitheft systems installed to begin with. It wouldn't be long now until her coffers would be full again; it was just a waiting game with these people, but it did stop Mr. Johnson from dropping in anymore. Charles kind of liked the guy but it was becoming a bit of a bother. At that point, Charles decided to dump the Caprice as it had drawn Mr. Johnson's attention at one point and Charles just told him it had quit running and the value of the car didn't warrant fixing it. He drove it out one night and parked it with the keys in it at the local convenience store and walked away. No one knew him personally or by his phony I.D. and there was no way to trace it back to him so as long as no one followed him home, he was off scot-free.

Of course, Benny's presence in the home had sparked a conversation with Mr. Johnson and he seemed more curious about that than almost anything else. But true to Banny's credo they kept it simple and Benny was just a long-time friend of Charles and Ida was gracious enough to allow him to rent a room from her in this great big house. A bit odd possibly but not an unheard-of situation. And so it was that the insurance finally came through only eight months after the burglary proving once again that one could actually make the insurance pay what they owed; it just depended on the capability of the client to out wait the big corporation.

Of course, it wasn't in cash, and they stipulated they would not do that again. But it was money in the bank and the investigation was closed at that point. Ida dropped the carrier the day the case closed and had only kept them to reduce suspicion. But unless they had rock solid evidence of fraud, there was nothing they could do at that point. Still, they watched for anyone staking out the place anytime they left the house. Ida never did tell them what she had done with her money and no matter how hard they tried; they couldn't weasel it out of her. But she never seemed to lack cash and they were pretty sure it was on the premises. But even they could not find it and they never did figure out where she went on the rare occasions she disappeared. It was a long-term mystery they would have to be patient to solve but at this point, they weren't interested in stealing her money anymore. All of them had their sites set much higher on what Lee Roy and his partners had waiting for them.

One evening as the three amigos sat around enjoying some very high-end liquors and a few shots of Tanqueray No. Ten. Ida finally admitted that she had most of the money hidden in a very secure location in the house but that was all the information she would give up. Aside from the money she had put down on the fourplex the rest of the millions were intact. And she'd taken most of what she needed from her bank account for the fourplex but only what was necessary to secure the mortgage and do the necessary cleanup required to make them top notch. She felt she had to make a money trail for the bank and the insurance carrier if she was to appear legit. Then she made a proposal to the boys that they were not expecting and it was so far off the life they had created together and had planned to pursue, that they were stunned. She suggested that they create a corporation of property ownership and begin a life on the straight and narrow.

CHAPTER NINE:
SHAKE AND BAKE

Except for in their scams the boys had never even considered going straight. There had just never been enough money in it to even consider. Between all the taxes, permits, licenses and inspections it had become almost impossible to make a go of going straight unless one was already super rich. If one involved investors, they generally took all of the gross out of it before it got to the person doing all of the leg work. But now Ida was talking a great deal of money between the three of them and the fourplex would be paid off when she received her money from the insurance and it had cleared her bank. A legitimate purchase from her ill-gotten gains that no one could contest.

Then she owned a piece of real-estate that would make a nice sum every month and there was no worry about interest, or taxes as that would simply be sitting in an account paid by the rent collected. Once she owned the fourplex outright, she could use that as collateral for her next purchase and not risk her home or the money she had stashed. She would be using the bank's money as a tool and not a crutch. If the boys followed suit, they had a cash reserve in the corporation that would convince any bank of a low interest real-estate loan which they'd pay off almost immediately thus laundering their cash and looking legit. They were beginning to understand the genius of her plan. A forensic accountant would likely figure it out in a heartbeat but there was no reason for that to come up as long as they kept their noses clean on taxes. Three years out and there would be no reason for the tax man to look anymore anyway. They'd be legit. But that tropical island still sounded so good… With legitimate money though, they could take a vacation.

It would likely be a good move to finally get out of the rat race of the con. It had been a long time since Jake Sullivan or Jim Benny had a permanent home and now that Jake was comfortable being Charles in a relationship he had never even hoped to have had, he was thinking this might not be a bad idea. He looked at Benny and then he looked Ida straight in the eye and told her they would need an iron clad contractual obligation spelling out each person's responsibility and gains upon dissolution. That was quite a mouthful in his inebriated condition. She looked him straight back and said, "Why Mr. Gordon, don't you trust me?"

Smiling broadly, he responded, "It's just business."

Jim had never shot gin from his nose before but he laughed that hard. They all laughed at Jim and his gin as it burned his sinuses, they were such good friends it almost seemed a shame to bring up business but Charles was right; it's just business. Friends stay friends when business stays business. Besides, it was almost time to execute the download from the partners backup computer and having an incorporation under which to hide the offshore accounts and even shell companies would make it a smidge harder to track the money. Ida knew just the attorney in Louisiana to help get them set up.

It took three weeks for Ida's attorney to get the paperwork put together and she was certain the boys would agree but she insisted they each get their own attorney to look it over. If they didn't, not only might it invalidate the agreement but they might find they could never trust each other again. It was imminently important that they trust each other. Since the day the boys had come clean with Ida, they'd had no reason to distrust each other and it would be a true shame to find they had a reason now. They had a love triangle of sorts of which Benny got none of the benefits but they were truly happy together. Especially when Benny shot gin out of his nose. It was a good time whenever they were together and not many friends could say that. And now they had a plan to carry that friendship forward with a financial goal they could all agree.

It took another three weeks for the boys' attorneys to get back to them with some minor proposed changes, another week for Ida's attorney to agree and make the changes and another week to schedule the notarized signing. By the time it was done they almost felt like they had been run through a ringer because they each had to sit down with their own attorney to go over everything. Jim didn't understand how those guys could do it day in and day out but that's why they were attorneys and he wasn't. His head was mess enough having a permanent memory of everything. During the interim, Benny set up the offshore accounts according to his attorney and a couple of shell companies to convolute the matter. It was almost a stroke... Not of brilliance but a real genuine stroke. It was a pile of paperwork in addition to everything else they were doing but Jim got it done and lived to tell about it. Tomorrow was Wednesday and Charles and Ida wanted to hit Lee Roy's stash. They had been unsuccessful in tracking down that of Kong and Vinny but Lee Roy's was good enough for Ida.

Benny had also been busy getting a bit of detcord and primers for the job and that was no easy task. Detcord had a burn rate of 21,000 feet per second and was used widely in the military but getting it out was a major work of magic. It left a highly transferable residual chemical trail and anyone handling it could be tracked and prosecuted. It could be had, but it was not easy to get. But Benny did it. He managed to get Twenty feet of the stuff and he could only hope it was enough. It should be but if it wasn't, Lee Roy would have a heck of a time getting to the money they'd be leaving behind as at the very least, that type of explosion would ruin the security on his little garage. He got a couple of the old silly putty eggs from a dollar type store to hold it in place and hoped it would be enough to do the job. He told Charles and Ida to try and stuff as much as they could into the cracks of the man door and the safe, they assumed was inside and wrap the rest around the locks. They didn't want to be anywhere nearby when they set it off because this stuff was worse than nitro glycerin.

Charles and Ida set off to the storage at five a.m. so they could be ahead of any traffic. It was just about two hours to get there if they heeded the speed limit and there was no reason to draw attention to themselves. A two-hour drive never seemed to take so long, it certainly hadn't the first time they made the drive. This time it was for real and they would either come back victorious or carried on their shields. Well, it sounded good in their heads when they were discussing it with Jim. It would, at the very least, be one hell of a fireworks display. Being four-hundred feet off the road and surrounded by scrub brush, they hoped it wouldn't be too terribly obvious.

When they arrived, they chose to park on the far side of the scrub brush in hopes no one would notice the Talon. Walking down to the door it appeared someone had found the place since they had been there last and had tried fruitlessly to jimmy the man door. That hadn't even come close to working and they could only hope they had enough power in their detcord to be enough. Charles found a suitable piece of wood to jam between the door frame and the door to widen the crack as much as possible and proceeded to jam as many layers of detcord into the crack she could fit. Then he withdrew the wedge. It was more than he expected and he had only seven feet left to wrap around the outside portion of the locks. If Benny was right about this stuff, the man door should be a breeze.

He placed the igniter and fuse over the crack in the door as that seemed the logical place to put it. He then lit the fuse and they ran to the top of the incline, turned left behind the scrub and covered their ears. Even as far as they were away from the explosion it knocked them on their butts and their ears still hurt even being covered. They picked themselves up off the ground and took note of the ample smoke cloud rising above them and when they looked down below, the explosion not only opened the door but took a chunk of the concrete side wall with it. Not completely but it was a sizable divot. That was one to Benny's credit. They went inside using their phones to light their way. There was Angelique's Camry under a car cover and at the far end was the safe they had expected to find. What they had not expected to find were the half dozen cardboard boxes filled with stacks of hundred-dollar bills. They had Lee Roy's stash in addition to his other stash and his other stash. It was like the movies depicting what a drug lord might have stacked inside his house's walls.

They moved the boxes of bills outside the door and proceeded to set the detcord on the safe. It was a shame but the Camry was going to take a beating. They needed extra time to get out the door and up the incline this time. They had no intention of being caught in this enclosed area with this blast and they didn't want an instant repeat of the last explosion. At least they wouldn't see a smoke cloud coming out of the door this time but that would be a heck of a thing to work in. They lit the fuse and ran. The ground still shook and the dust coming out the door was far more than they had expected but it wasn't nearly as catastrophic as it had been the time before. The door had come off its hinges and bounced off the wall and down the side of the Camry. What a shame, it had been a nice car although this many years down the road it had lost value for sitting unused. But there was no money inside the safe. It was filled with gold ingots. That Lee Roy was one smart cookie to invest in precious metal.

The back seats of the Talon folded inward and down making the hatch area very roomy. Ida and Charles caried the very heavy boxes of cash up the incline and stacked them in the back of the car. They left the few half full boxes till last but carried those up and left them accessible to put the gold ingots in. Those ingots were not light, two hands full were all either of them could carry at once and they made at least ten trips each. By the time they had everything the back of the Talon was hanging low and it felt a bit obvious they had an overloaded vehicle. What could they do? It was what they had to make the trip. They closed the boxes and got the heck out of Dodge. Just off the highway they spied a small gas stop that appeared to have a lot of trinkets and such and they pulled in. Ida went inside and bought a Mexican blanket and jumped back into the car. As Charles drove, Ida reached back and put the blanket over the top of the boxes to hide them out a bit. In their excitement it was hard not to speed but they kept it slow and mellow, they said hardly a word on the way back.

Ida finally broke the silence and called Jim, "It's time, download the backup drives and take every cent they have."
"It will be my pleasure, my lady."

The culmination of the plan almost felt criminal to Charles and Ida's mood reflected that it was a red-letter moment for her. It was mostly the adrenaline working on them but that would subside. It was going to be chaos at the front office for the next few hours and they would be trying to figure out what happened with the computers going nuts on them. It wouldn't be obvious at first but sooner or later someone would notice the internet was overloaded and then it might dawn on them. Benny had their accounts emptied first and then the information coming to him and file after file automatically being emailed to the FBI. They would be going crazy trying to figure out what was coming in to them and then just for general purposes, Benny would send them copies of everything on Blu-ray disc hard copies. Funny thing about having rotating ISPs, at the top of each file was the name of the company and its address. Not just the front office but every one of their satellites also. The partners had thought it was a touch of professionalism, that's not at all how it would work out for them.

Within hours there were news reports of something going on with the police and the FBI involved, a shootout, dozens dead, a warehouse full of drugs and a dozen warrants being sought for accomplices. A crazy man shouting to reporters, "I'm going to find you Charles! You're a dead man Charles!"
As they unloaded the boxes from the Talon Charles excused himself for a moment and came back out with champaign and three glasses. The gate to the drive was closed and locked and he didn't feel self-conscience about taking a moment They all sat on the front step to the porch and toasted, "to us!"
He and Ida finally relaxed after their harrowing and explosive experience. The drive back was especially tense as although not likely, they could have been pulled over for an overloaded vehicle and then all hell would have broken loose. Anything over ten thousand dollars in one person's possession is automatically

considered drug money and immediately confiscated. The cops would have had a field day with all that cash and gold. And technically they'd have been right, but it wasn't drug money any more, it wasn't stolen drug money. Try explaining that one to a jury of your peers, they'd convict a person just out of jealousy.

The three finished off that bottle of champaign and went back to their task. The gold would go into Ida's safe; the cash would have to be stored in the safe room for now and they would launder it into property as they had the chance. Ida finally showed the boys where she kept her money, it was brilliant because it was so hidden it didn't even need to be locked up. Besides, now the boys had more than enough they wouldn't need hers and they were incorporated. They would each keep a bit of their own but eventually, most all the funds would end up accounted for. Not quite all, they weren't stupid, but if they were going to be legit, they had to be legit.

Once they had the boxes all into the safe room, Ida closed the door with them inside. She backed up against the door and in her most sultry voice she said, "Come here boys, I've got something to show you." Behind the door she pressed the white wood panel wall and it went click, click. The panel opened outward; it was completely invisible until it did. Behind that, a sliding door with a small latch to hold it in place. Moving that aside and reaching in, Ida turned on the light in the room. There were shelves and shelves of cash and gold ingots, even more that what Lee Roy had stashed. It was an amazing little room and the boys were beside themselves...

"All this time and we had no idea!" exclaimed Benny.

Ida laughed, "I've always been two steps ahead of you both. What do you say we get these moved into the room here where we know they'll be safe."

She chuckled and the boys hardly missed a beat. That was no problem by them.

CHAPTER TEN:
LEGITIMACY

The time for researching real properties for purchase was now upon them. They didn't need to move particularly fast but they wanted to make a splash in the local market before any whales took note of them and bought up everything that was still affordable. They felt that apartments and town homes would be wise investments because they were multi-family and the economy wouldn't hurt their income as badly if the bottom dropped out. Benny went to work finding several that would be in good areas with higher income tenants. Those would eventually go by the wayside as so many did over time it was just the natural progression of real estate. For now, they would produce a sizable income and if they could buy enough of them before anyone took notice, the values would rise accordingly once the whales jumped in the water. It was the best way they could reason to get in quick and protect their investment at the same time. If the values jumped too high and the taxes outweighed the advantages, they could sell one or more of the more highly taxed properties and move their assets elsewhere. It really was a game of chess.

Many of the properties that were available were way overpriced but they had also been on the market far too long; some for years. Benny expanded their search further from town, he didn't like doing that as the best properties were near downtown Dallas but some of the areas around Little Elm and Frisco showed good growth and there was a lot of retail business that was prospering in addition to many large corporations going in to avoid the higher taxes of Dallas city proper. Dallas was land locked and had little room for expansion except up and that was the direction of taxes, unfortunately. Texas had no income tax but the municipalities sucked people dry through property tax and the larger the cities, the higher taxes grew.

While Benny was busy with that task and it was a task, to be sure, Charles drove back to his mother's house in Louisiana. It was occupied by squatters, mostly drug addled and homeless urchins. He chased them all out with a loud voice, a bat and the threat of a police presence. He needed them gone so he could dig up the several tin boxes he had stashed around the tiny property. It was all he had left of his mother but it was time to raze it. The windows were all broken out, the roof was rotten and it stank of mold.

Once he had found and retrieved his boxes there, he called a local realtor and had her meet him and he nearly gave her the property under the promise to raze it. He didn't ever want to come back for any reason large or small. Although his memories were not terrible it was a place he never wanted to see again. She even had the cash to buy it for the pittance for which he was willing to sell it. It was nothing but a memory and even though it was the last vestige of his mother, he was finally ready to let it go.

He proceeded to his home base in Arkansas. His home away from the road was a little log cabin in the woods with one window and one door. It was wired for electric if he wanted it but he mostly used a generator when he actually stayed there; he preferred to live off grid when he could. It had a natural artesian well springing from the hill side behind it and that ran into a cistern and overflowed into a small lake he'd hand dug out front. The cistern fed his cabin after a filter to keep debris out of his few sink pipes and a water heater for the shower. He had a TV that he seldom used, a Citizens Band radio just in case he wanted to chat with some of the locals that he'd never even met and a small FM radio CD combo for his favorite tunes; most of which he kept on his phone these days. It was funny he considered the people on the CB to be locals. They lived much like he did in his cabin, only they did it full time. Most were at least a mile away as near as he could tell and some much further by their descriptions.

A small sign on the front door said, "If you use my cabin while I'm away, please leave it as you found it." He never locked it and had never found it used or abused. Of course, not many, if at all, had a clue it was back here but if anyone had found it, they'd been kind. On occasion he felt there might be hope for humanity; not much, but a little. Who was he to judge? He still felt a bit queer about what he'd done to the partners. He had no idea why. He just liked the guys; was he getting soft in his maturity? He had taken on the cardinal sin of partners, fallen in love and found a conscience. The triple whammy for the end of a con man. He figured it was probably good that Ida had talked them into becoming a real-estate holding company. Even so, he was tired and conflicted and decided to stay a night in his cabin that he enjoyed so much. It was away from the world and it gave his mind ease.

He called and talked with Ida for almost an hour getting an update on what Benny had found. He talked to her about his misgivings; he knew in his head that the partners had deserved it but it wasn't right to withhold his conscience from the woman that had suffered from Lee Roy's treachery. Not to mention the hit he'd put out on Benny. He let Ida know he was staying the night to clear his head and get some rest before making the long drive back to Dallas. At least Ida was understanding about it. She seemed to see right through to his very soul and he supposed that's why he truly felt an emotional bond with her. Right now, all he wanted to do was to sleep and then be back at her side with his best friend, his only other friend that he trusted. Tomorrow he would move the wood stove and retrieve his cash from under it. Everyone had their own version of the underground.

Morning broke early at five a.m. as the sun blazed through the East facing window of the cabin. Charles wasn't feeling it this morning but he knew he had to get in a couple of cups of coffee and get that stove out of the way. The morning hours in the hill country were a bit brisk any time of year so he dawned his jacket until he would be working up a sweat. He turned on the electric just for this morning so he could brew a pot of coffee and turned on the morning radio talk and music show of the local rock and roll station. They always had some fun banter going on amongst the four personalities and this morning was no different. Today they were talking about the huge drug ring from out in Dallas, which had been all over the news for over a week now, and how the FBI was looking for a man named Charles driving a dark green Eagle Talon; wanted for questioning in the matter. That wasn't good if he was going to be transporting his cash on the interstate. They would confiscate his loot and ask questions for years before they gave it back; if ever they did. He sure didn't want to dump his sweet ride so soon but he probably needed to do that. He unloaded the tins he'd dug up at his mother's place and slid them under the bed.

He gave Ida a call and let her know what was going on and that he would be later than expected. He drove the Talon out the long gravel access road that stretched for what must have been three miles. He would have just left the Talon parked at the cabin and walked out but it was another five miles on the two-lane highway to town once he reached it. It had cost him more than a fortune to run the electric out to the cabin but it had been well worth it. The privacy was priceless and he never once had encountered another human being out there. His neighbors on the CB radio felt the same way about their places as they all had lived there a long time; decades for some as he understood it. Purchasing the fifty acres he had, was almost nothing back fifteen years ago but he could only imagine the cost today. It was now considered premium land. Charles parked his little disposable hot rod beside the highway a quarter mile from town and started walking. If anyone asked, he'd tell them he ran out of gas.

When he got to town he saw just what he might be able to afford in an older S-Ten Chevy Blazer It was the newer (1999), smaller, more gas friendly version of the old full size blazer but it still had the room he needed to carry a load back to Dallas. The paint had buffed out almost like new and the interior was brand new. It had a posted price tag of $12,000.00 and that was more than he was willing to pay on the older vehicle. He figured what the heck? Nothing ventured, nothing gained. Walking in like he owned the place he told them he'd like to take the truck for a test drive. No small talk, not a request but almost a demand. Said with a smile of course, one catches more bees with honey than with vinegar. One salesman jumped like his family was starving so Charles allowed him to get the keys for him. James asked if he could ride along, it would save the time of copying identification.

James had caught on that Charles was in a bit of a hurry. James just became Charles best friend; for the moment. He was probably around twenty-five and didn't seem new to the business. He hinged his sales technique on knowing his inventory the ups and downs of each model. He asked Charles what had attracted him to the S-10 version of the Blazer instead of some of the newer off shoots like the Trail Blazer. James mentioned to Charles that this unit had a limited slip Posi traction rear end that might help with the snow and hill country around here. Charles told James that this particular blazer had the 262CID V6 which had lots of power but still got a respectable twenty miles to the gallon according to some of the magazines. It could actually haul a small trailer and had plenty of cargo space for his needs.

Charles didn't need to take it for a long test drive, it started like a champ, didn't blow any smoke and it didn't rattle driving on a bumpy road. He found what he needed and now he just had to get the price where he wanted it. He looked James directly in the eye and said, "James, you know that price is well above book for a vehicle that old. I agree it's looking really good inside and out and it sems to be there mechanically. What can you do for me to make it follow me home?"

"I might be able to get the manager to come down five-hundred."

"Now, James. That isn't even a starting point for me. If I was to sell it in a week, I'd need to get my money back in full. Now I don't expect you to give it to me but if you want a sale today, this moment, go ask your manager what you can do for me to say, 'Thank you very much.'"

James walked into the manager's office and the manager walked back in with him. Of course, the manager was full of smiles and an outstretched hand calling Charles his friend. It was standard sales tactics and Charles had seen it a thousand times. They all knew it was a 'Good enough' vehicle on any note or cash lot. And these guys were just trying to eke out a living in a small town. Charles couldn't fault them for trying.

"All right guys, here's the scoop. That '99 model right there, books at between seven and eight thousand." Their faces went slack. "It wholesales for around four thousand. I would pay eight for that all day long in the big city. I don't blame you for trying to make a living but you have what I want and I'm willing to pay a premium price; just not that premium price. I want you two to take a moment to think it over in your office over there, but I'm willing to pay ten thousand cash today, on the spot if I can drive it away. If you can't do that, we walk away friends and I'll go to the lot down the road a piece and see what they can do for me. Take five minutes and let me know."

The two walked away toward the office but stopped short. Charles had put on his best smiling face for the occasion and didn't necessarily expect his strong-arm tactic to work but he got lucky. The manager went back to his office and James came back and took the deal. Charles was on his way in half an hour and everybody knew they'd gotten the best deal they could expect that day.

Driving back to his property he knew he'd dodged a bullet as he drove past his Talon over which a County Mounty was making a fuss. There was nothing to connect him to the car so Charles wasn't worried but he did breathe a sigh of relief. He drove on to the gravel road and the three miles up that road to his cabin and sat in the blazer for a few minutes to see if the law would find him curious enough to bother with. He checked his watch and realized he'd already lost three hours of the day and he still had a three-hour drive home. At least he wouldn't hit Dallas traffic going up the DNT from IH-635. That was always brutal. He was convinced the po-po had no interest in him so he backed the blazer up to the door and hopped out to make the transfer of funds. So to speak. He moved the wood stove aside and started pulling box after box of hundreds from under the floor. He wasn't sure it was as much as Ida had but it was a respectable weight in paper. He had the last box loaded in along with the tins from his mother's place and covered it with a blanket from his bed there in the cabin and as he closed up the back, who should come quietly up his drive but the County Mounty.

Charles just about choked but he knew the officer had no clue what was up. The man got out of his cruiser and told Charles he was wondering if anyone had come wandering by. "I've never known who owned this place, would that be you?"

"Well, yes sir. I've owned it for quite a few years."

"Would you happen to have some I.D.?"

"Yes, I do."

"May I see it?"

"Is there a problem, am I in trouble, sheriff?"

"No, not at this time. I just like to know who I'm dealing with."

"My name is Jake Sullivan, Sir."

"May I see your I.D.?"

"Sir, I have identified myself. You came on my property uninvited and you want to see my I.D. I've told you who I am and although I respect the police, I'm not obliged to speak to you anymore because now, in my opinion, you are abusing our authority. Please leave."

"Look, I don't have anything against you. Why don't you do this the easy way and just show me your I.D.?"

"What's that name tag? Granby? Sheriff Granby, you are here uninvited and I have asked you to leave. You are now guilty of criminal trespass."

"Turn around and put your hands behind your back."

"Leave."

The officer went for his taser and Jake throat punched him, then shoved his fingers in his eyes and kicked him in the eggs. The man went down and that set off his automatic alert over his radio that an officer was down. Jake had no choice at this point if he wanted to remain a free man. The sheriff had nothing on him until he defended himself against a false arrest. But now it was his word against that of the county sheriff. Nobody would believe him, especially with millions in cash in the back of a recently cash purchased Blazer with fake I.D. and a green Eagle Talon parked just down the road a couple of miles. Jake drew the officer's weapon and shot him. Four times in the back, until he quit moving. Then one more time in the head. He stood there for a moment transfixed over the body not believing what he had just done. He knew he had no choice as he would have been arrested and held indefinitely under suspicion of drug involvement or at the very least some type of money laundering.

He had to get out of town, he would be a person of interest as soon as his description was known and having bought a vehicle for cash, that would be the description of a person of interest. Jake kept the officer's weapon although that would not be for long. He jumped into the Blazer and started it, He calmed himself as much as possible. The last thing he wanted to do was tear out of there and bring attention to himself when he hit the two-lane. Then it hit him, the dash cam had him dead to rights unless the officer turned it off. He couldn't take that chance. He jumped back out of the vehicle and shot the shit out of the DVR. It was mounted right up front where it was easily accessible. He grabbed the vest camera off the corps and threw it into the Blazer. He would dispose of that and the weapon when he crossed over the red river. It wasn't flowing very heavily but it was enough that it would ruin any DNA or video evidence.

Now he had to go. It wasn't likely that anyone had heard more than a poacher firing at some game animal but the officer may have radioed his position to the dispatcher. And if someone put two and two together, they might already be heading his direction. He could move fairly fast down the gravel road but once he got to the two-lane, he'd have to mind his Ps and Qs, as his mother used to say. He thought his heart would beat out of his chest. He'd never killed a man before; it was almost instinctive. He knew he had no other choice with a sheriff that was obviously crooked. He knew he could never win against law enforcement that would lie. He was sweating bullets now and he wished he'd not put on the jacket. It was covered in blood splatter and he needed to remove and dispose of it but now wasn't the time. He turned on the air conditioner. He checked his face in the rear-view mirror and could see some splatter, he'd have to deal with that as well. He had dead man's blood on his face... He felt sick to his stomach but he couldn't allow that now. He had to put miles between himself and the cabin. Unless they were able to recover any of the video, which was doubtful, they had nothing to connect him now but his proximity and the fact they could prove he was in town. If they couldn't find him, they had nothing. If he could make it through Texarkana, he would be home free.

He was approaching the red river and the traffic was light which was good for him, he could roll down the window and throw the incriminating evidence out as he crossed over. He pulled the jacket off over his head as he drove but he'd need to wait until he refueled to toss that. As he crossed over the Red River, he hit the button to let the right window down and let fly with the nine-millimeter Glock and then the vest camera; they both went over the rail. That much was done and no one was the wiser. He probably should have crushed the camera but it was too late now. Water would have that corroded beyond repair in a couple of days. And the river would likely have washed it miles downstream. His fuel situation would not allow him to travel past the first gas station as he entered into Texarkana so he pulled off the highway on the egress ramp. He drove slowly through the parking lot of the truck stop and spotted out a bum by the trash dumpsters looking for some food. Charles stopped and scratched the now dried blood from his face and it came off easily.

Once his face was clean, he pulled up to a pump and filled up, with no ATM card he had to go in and put money on the pump to get it activated but that was not unusual at these places and no one seemed to take notice of him. Once he had fuel, he looked for the bum and drove on around to him and rolled down his window. He'd bought a hot dog and a piece of pizza for himself and the same for his new found best buddy by the dumpsters. He rolled up to the man and the man lowered his head and tried to slink away. Hey partner! Don't go! I've got something here for you. The man stopped and looked at him warily. So many mean people would do that and then dump their garbage or say something truly mean. Not many ever did anything good for him. Charles handed the man the food first and the jacket second. He told him to take care and drove away slowly. He could hear the man yell, "God bless you sir!" And Charles hoped he would, greatly. God knew he needed it, especially now that he was a murderer.

He headed back out to the access road and hit the Ingress ramp to enter the highway at speed unlike most drivers. That's what the ramps were for, getting up to speed. So many people were too stupid to understand that small concept. Charles was amazed they had passed a driver's exam. It was only a few minutes before he entered the State of Texas mid-way through Texarkana, A city on the state line with two different governments and police forces. He breathed a sigh of relief as that would add a factor of difficulty for the law to track him if they ever did try. It also made him a federal fugitive if ever it came to that. With any luck, he would never hear of the incident again but only time would tell. At that point he knew it was just under three hours to be back at home, safe and warm in the arms of his lover and in the company of his best friend; the only two people in the world he trusted and considered to be his friends.

The drive back to Dallas was mundane at this point and he felt encouraged when he made the interchange to go North on IH-635 after the morning rush and just in front of the noon lunch hour congestion. Positioning himself in the center lane it should be a smooth ride home. It took only a half hour from that point and he was pulling into the drive at Ida's house. He had called to let her know he was on his way once he crossed the Red River and had hinted to the trouble he'd found himself in, but promised he'd tell them both the whole story once he got back. He had barely processed all the details in his own head even now. He couldn't believe the sheriff had bullied him and wanted to arrest him on nothing at all. Most sheriffs were big believers in the law and especially the constitution, but every aspect of government was so conflagrated these days one couldn't count on righteousness or justice from any quarter.

Ida and Jim were quick to help him unload because he wouldn't say anything about the trip out to Arkansas until the job was done and stored in the closet in the safe room. Charles wanted everything stashed just in case anything else could go wrong with the not so perfect, perfect plan. Charles wanted a drink. He didn't generally imbibe that early in the day but these circumstances were surreal and he was still shaking just a bit just thinking about it. The experience would leave him a different man and he could feel the real change in his entire body. Jim and Ida refused the alcoholic relaxant as they sat listening to Charles tale, first of dumping the Talon and then of buying the Blazer. What bad luck to have the report go out that morning in the area and the sheriff finding the car almost immediately. Normally, there weren't enough sheriff's patrols in the counties to be johnny on the spot like that.

Both of his friends decided to join him in that drink after hearing of how the situation went down. It just wasn't a normal situation no matter how one looked at it and it was obvious that things would have turned out badly had Charles not taken the actions that had transpired. There wasn't any reason for the sheriff to act the way he did, they wondered if he'd been under some kind of pressure or what might have had that effect on the man's judgement. They all kept thinking it simply wasn't normal.

Jim had found several properties that they needed to look at right away and they decided to take a ride in the Blazer to do just that. It would be good to confirm the ones they wanted to buy and to get everyone's mind off of the dead sheriff; at least for now. Jim had done a good job of picking very workable properties, some needed some superficial work and they didn't even bother going inside at this point, they needed to get bids in on them that quickly to avoid alerting the whales in the industry. They had all been on the market for six months or more so there were bound to be some issues with some of them but Jim had been sure to locate the best neighborhoods so they could recover any losses in short order. His research showed that most of them had been purchased by small fries that didn't seem to have the capital to make it work and the banks were nipping at their heals for the payments. Several were showing in foreclosure on the DallasCAD.org web page.

After they had spent the afternoon confirming the potential purchases, they rolled by Benny's house to gather the last of his belongings and wealth stash. Benny didn't have or need much. Some of what was there he decided just to leave rather than try to consolidate it with what they all had together or store it somewhere. It wasn't worth his time or trouble since the download of the partner's wealth. They were all sitting on a pile of money and even more than they had perceived possible. It was good to be truly wealthy. Most of Jim's wealth remaining at the house was actually in gold ingots so converting it and depositing what he needed into the property holding company should be a breeze and they could start the purchase process right away. Their only issue was carrying it out to the Blazer because it was quite heavy and he had nosey neighbors. There was no fence in the front yard of his rental home so they backed up to the front door but of course that didn't stop his neighbors from sticking their noses in. What a pain!

When they finished, the Blazer was packed to the gills and Benny had to ride on the jockey box between Charles and Ida. Not his idea of a good time and he whined incessantly about it the entire way home. At least it wasn't the e-brake handle! He just wouldn't shut up! It was early evening by that time and the three of them unloaded only the gold and what little cash Jim left here at the house still, to the closet upstairs. They parked the blazer where the Talon used to sit, ordered some pizza and called it a day. Now it was time for some serious drinks to celebrate the next steps in creating their legitimacy. They called up a property agent that Ida knew to get their purchases started come the morning. Benny didn't want to handle this under his phony license as they were going to be too legit to quit so they opted to actually pay someone to do the job right.

Ida was keeping tabs on the courts and Lee Roy's incarceration to be sure he was being secured without any chance of the case being dropped. There was too much evidence for that, but stranger things had happened in the past to other criminals. Mostly in making deals for leniency. The last thing they needed was for Lee Roy to show up on Ida's door step, they knew that would be their last day on planet earth. Of course, he couldn't know of her involvement as she really had none except to employ the boys to get the goods on him. But they did live with her and there could somehow be a trail of which they had not thought to cover their tracks. A trial date had been set but it was months in the future and they would not give Ida any explanation as to why it was so far out. The three sufficed to be patient while the Feds built their case against him and his cohorts, they could afford to be patient here on the outside and the partners had no access to bail money.

The next day the property agent wanted to come over and meet them at their home but the three of them didn't really want anyone to know where they actually lived. They agreed to meet for lunch at a restaurant local to the agent and themselves and there gave the information on the properties to Zelda Oggeldorff. Seriously? Okay, they could blame her parents for that one. She told them to call her Zee. Zee was a relatively attractive blonde, fifty something lady that was probably quite beautiful in her younger days. Time takes its toll on us all and her personality was such that she seemed more lovely than she appeared. That was actually a very good thing for someone who depended on clients to make a living. The boys liked her immediately and they hit it off quite well.

They sat in the booth of the restaurant and Jim went over the properties showing her the notes he'd made on each printout from Dallas Central Appraisal District. It wasn't a long meeting and she closed by asking them how much they had to put down on each of the ten properties they had given her to work on. She almost pulled it off but couldn't quite keep from choking just a bit when Ida replied, "We will be paying by check."
"Well, that is certainly not normal, will that be secured funds?"
"That will be a company check. They can wait for the funds to clear."

"I see. That may not be to their liking."

Ida responded, "Although we want the seller to be happy, they will be happy with the money no matter how we give it to them, let them know they can have however much earnest money is required to get the job done. That should sweeten the pot."

"How would you feel about a direct transfer of funds, bank to bank?"

"If they don't mind absorbing the bank charges on such a transfer, that's fine."

"Oh, that's not how it's usually done."

"We are willing to work with the owners as much as possible, but they will accept our terms and absorb any charges we might incur trying to please them."

"Oh, well, if you insist."

"We do. We don't mind bending over backwards but if it means we have to pay charges, they need to absorb those charges."

"I'll see what I can do."

"I'm sure you'll do just fine," responded Ida.

Zee was finally done with that conversation and the group parted ways. She had been quite nice about the whole discussion but Ida was absolutely brutal about making any wish possible, just at the seller's expense.

As soon as they knew the seller's requirements, which would take a few days, they would transfer the necessary funds to their stateside bank. Then two weeks to get the funds into the states. The transfer was actually instantaneous but the banks liked making their interest on any transfer before releasing the finds. They liked to say it was to ensure there were no issues with the transfer but that was just poppycock. It was final as soon as someone pressed the enter key. Just like taking the money from the partners, it was over almost before it was done. Charles wasn't feeling as badly about the whole affair with Lee Roy, Kong and Vinny the more separated he was from it. Especially with his more recent experience with the sheriff. That had rocked his world and he was doing his best to put it behind him. There had been nothing on the news in Dallas and the three were assuming it was now water under the bridge, Red River water.

It did not take as long as they had expected for the property owners to come back with counter offers. Many were motivated to get the deal done and no one wanted anything outlandish so the deals were agreed upon and the money made good. The group would soon own ten properties that should be able to provide income and legitimacy for them and they could make a life for themselves right here in the states. Buying ten properties cash was also going to make every other property holding company sit back and take notice and they might come under investigation if they tried to buy anything more. They would have to be patient before moving any further. That would also give them time to make the necessary improvements on properties to get top dollar from the rent.

It was another month before they could close on all the properties and it seemed terribly long and at times like someone was keeping a foot on the brake to slow things down. They hired a property manager and a construction company to bring everything up to snuff. That was another month for some of the properties but they had an occupancy rate of 97% before long and trending higher. Their holding company name sometimes raised eyebrows but it wasn't long before all the movers and shakers new about them. Their little stunt of buying so many properties all at once made a noticeable blip in local values and they were right to keep things under their hats until the moment of execution. It seemed to make a real impression around town and they were suddenly popular and invited to parties among the elite. Most of which they turned down.

The trial for Lee Roy finally came up on the docket and although they didn't go every day, Ida insisted the three of them show up on the day of sentencing. She had changed her mind about Lee Roy finding out who was responsible because the D.A was asking for twenty-five to life; she wanted to pour salt into the wound and neither of the boys could blame her. It had been a fairly high-profile case so the courtroom was packed with reporters and local authorities that had been involved. The three weren't noticeable sitting four rows back from the convicted drug kingpin. When he was led in, he didn't look up, he knew he was going away for a very long time and his heart was heavy knowing it all started when he tried to rob Max. Max who had died after giving him a chance to support his family, to give them a good life. Kong and Vinny had already been sentenced and they had received fifteen years before they were eligible for parole. His mind went back to Clitoris, Peckerwood and Rogers Rabbit, the wood chipper and Jean. He almost wept when Angelique and his momma torn up on the tracks crossed his mind. His life was over and he knew the judge would not go easy on him.

The judge made it as hard as possible on Lee Roy as he sat there ready to hear the sentence. He made it as long and drawn out as possible so that Lee Roy squirmed in his discomfort waiting, eternal waiting as this judge droned on about what a terrible person he was. All of the crimes for which he'd been responsible; all the lives his enterprise had likely affected. How much that taking out his operation had reduced crime in Dallas and the surrounding areas. Lee Roy couldn't help but wonder what the judge had his fingers into and if he would ever be held accountable. He knew that would never happen. The judge finally got down to the nitty gritty and in all seriousness said, "Prisoner stand for sentencing."

Lee Roy looked at him and sat there staring at the judge, he had no intention of standing.

"Bailiff, if the prisoner does not stand for sentencing, taze him and lay him up on the table."

Lee Roy flipped the judge off, he would let the bailiff taze him, he didn't care. He got exactly that. He was barely conscience when the judge continued and the reporters had a huge end to their stories.

"Prisoner, you are hereby sentenced to thirty-five years in a maximum-security facility and will not be eligible for parole for twenty-five years."

The courtroom erupted into cheers and the three sat there as Ida wept. Max was finally avenged. It was everything for which she could have hoped. Charles and Jim both put their arms around her. The courtroom started to clear out.

"Bailiff, remand the prisoner into custody."

The bailiff put the cuffs on Lee Roy and stood him up.

At that moment, Ida pulled herself together and encouraged the boys to stand with her behind Lee Roy. The three stood in silence and looked at him as the bailiff told him to move out. That's when he noticed them, standing there together, "YOU! YOU! I will kill all of you! You are dead, you just don't know it yet!" He struggled to get at them and they stood there in silence knowing he never would get to them. They wondered if he knew that he'd financed their startup into legitimacy? With that, they turned to leave as the bailiff subdued Lee Roy with another shot from the taser. He pissed himself and had to be carried out.

And so began their legitimacy and the Above the Law Realty, Inc.

The end.

Made in the USA
Columbia, SC
04 July 2024

f0e20c2f-e3fa-4b3e-a618-817b0de9fa93R01